A DOG'S PURPOSE

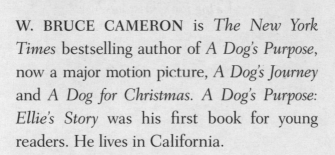

Bailey's Story

W. BRUCE CAMERON is *The New York Times* bestselling author of *A Dog's Purpose,* now a major motion picture, *A Dog's Journey* and *A Dog for Christmas. A Dog's Purpose: Ellie's Story* was his first book for young readers. He lives in California.

Also by
W. Bruce Cameron

A Dog's Purpose: Ellie's Story
A Dog's Purpose
A Dog's Journey
A Dog for Christmas

A DOG'S PURPOSE

Bailey's Story

W. Bruce Cameron

MACMILLAN CHILDREN'S BOOKS

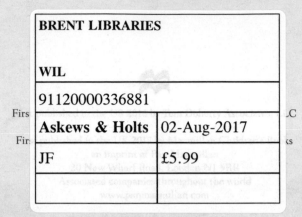
First ~~published~~ ...LC

First ~~...~~ ...s

ISBN 978-1-5098-5363-2

1 3 5 7 9 8 6 4 2

A CIP catalogue record for this book is available from
the British Library.

Printed and bound by CPI Group (UK) Ltd, Croydon CR0 4YY

For C ett a d!
We he to

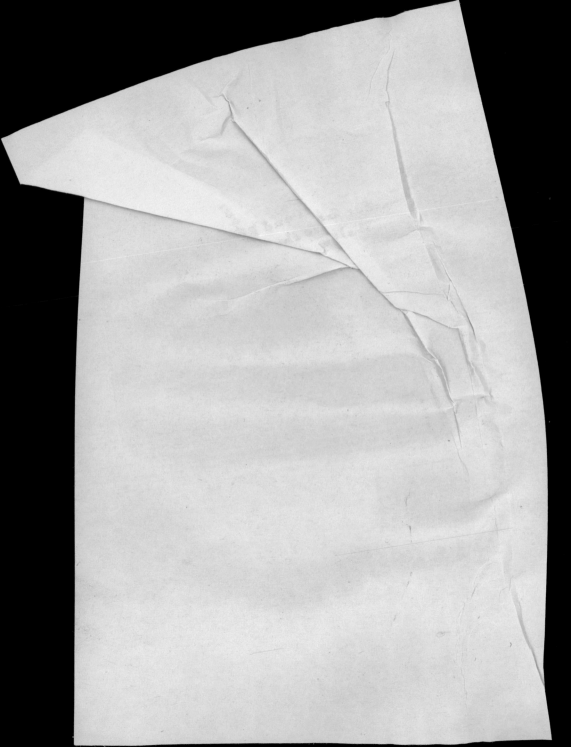

1

One day it occurred to me that the warm, squeaky, smelly things squirming around next to me were my brothers and sisters. I was very disappointed.

For a little while now, I had been pushing and shoving those wiggling objects aside so that I could get at my mother's furry warmth and her rich, delicious milk. So those things that had been getting in the way of my food were other puppies like me!

I blinked up at my mother, silently asking her to please get rid of the rest. I wanted her all to myself.

But she didn't. It seemed that my brothers and sisters were here to stay.

In that case, I decided, I was going to be the one in

charge. But my littermates didn't seem to understand. I'd try to grab one by the back of the neck, and two or three others would jump on top of *me*. By the time I'd shaken them off, the pup I'd been trying to teach a lesson to would be wrestling with someone else. If I tried a menacing growl, all my brothers and sisters just growled joyously back.

So irritating.

When I wasn't trying to make my littermates understand how the world worked, I'd explore a little. From the first, I could hear a lot of barking, and I smelt other dogs nearby. When I crawled out of a pile of siblings to see what I could see, the surface beneath my paws was rough and hard, and after a few steps my nose bumped into a wire fence. I was in a cage with a cement floor.

On the other side of the wire there were more puppies. These were not blond with dark eyes, like my siblings and my mother and me. They were tiny, energetic little guys with dark markings and hair that stuck up all over the place. They looked like they might be fun to play with, but that wire was between us.

When I turned around to look at the cage on the opposite side, I saw a female dog, white with black spots. Her belly hung down near the floor, and she moved slowly. She gave me one glance but didn't seem very interested.

On a third side of the cage there was a door. I'd noticed that door before. Every day a man would come by with a bowl of food for my mother, and he'd open the door and put the food in. She would get to her feet, shake off a puppy or two, and gulp her meal down, coming back to us as quickly as she could.

This was the first time I had taken a close look at what was beyond that door. Grass. A long strip of lawn that teased my nose with the smells of moist earth and growing things. Around the lawn was a wooden fence.

It was a lot to take in. I stumbled back to my mother and settled down for a nap on top of two sisters.

The next day, when the man came by, I was paying attention. He had a bowl of food in one hand and a piece of paper in the other, and he was frowning at it.

'Yorkshire terriers, week or so,' he said, looking in the cage next door, the one with the puppies. Then he stopped in front of our cage and peered inside it. 'Golden retrievers, probably three weeks yet, and got a dalmatian ready to pop any day.'

I could tell that he was not saying those words to any of the dogs. He never spoke to us. Quickly, he opened the door of our cage. I trotted over, eager to see what that green grass might feel like under my feet. But the man pushed me aside with a grunt, not very roughly, but not gently either. He put the bowl down in front of my mother.

Then he swung the door shut.

I tried to get a taste of what was in that bowl, but my mother nudged me away with her nose. It didn't smell as nice as milk, anyway. The man moved on, coming back with more bowls in his hands. He put the bowls of food down in the grass and went to the cage on our right. He opened the door, and then he did something that surprised me – he left it open! The puppies with the wiry fur – terriers, the man had called them – tumbled out on to the grass.

'No, not you,' the man said to their mother, pushing her back from the door the way he had pushed me.

I watched jealously as those little fur balls romped all over the grass. Their mother whimpered quietly behind her closed door. The man walked away, leaving the yard by a gate in the wooden fence while the puppies rolled on the grass and bit it and barked at it. One peed on it, and then everybody else of course had to sniff that spot carefully.

Then one of the puppies discovered a bowl of food by falling face-first into it. He came up with a snort, licked sticky brown glop from his nose, and fell in again. All of his brothers and sisters crowded around and did the same thing.

After the food was gone, the puppies came over to our cage door to sniff us. I licked at the leftover food on their faces while one of my brothers stood on my head. Then they left us to run up and down the grass, barking, tripping, getting back up. I saw that there were more cages to the left and to the right. The puppies raced up and down, sniffing the noses of every dog they could reach.

I wished I could be out there with them. I had explored as much as I could inside our little cage, with its smells of mother and puppies, food and milk. I was ready for more.

When the man came back into the yard, he left the gate open behind him. I could see a tiny sliver of blue sky, green trees, and dark roadway beyond. Longing seized me. There was something out there for me – I knew it. Something important. Something that I needed. If I were ever running free in the grass, I would head right out of that open gate. I couldn't understand why the terrier puppies didn't, but they were all too busy wrestling.

The man scooped up two puppies, one in each hand, and carried them out through the gate. He made two more trips for the rest. And then they were gone.

The yard was suddenly awfully quiet without all of their tiny, high-pitched barks. Their mother put her paws up on the gate and cried. Then she dropped down to pace back and forth.

The man came by her cage and looked at her, but

he didn't call out to her, didn't speak to her, didn't reach inside to touch her. Somehow I knew that he could have done those things, and that it would have helped to ease her unhappiness. But he didn't. He just turned and walked away.

The sadness of the mother in the cage next door made me sad as well. I burrowed back into the pack of my brothers and sisters, safe against my own mother's warm side.

But the thought of that gate into the outside world did not leave me. When our turn came to be let out on to the green grass, some days later, I was ready.

The man set down bowls of food for us, just as he'd done for the terriers, and he opened the gate to our cage. We rushed out on to the grass. Two sisters walked right over my head to get at the food bowls. I pushed my way between them and ate my fill. It was delicious, and it felt so satisfying to chew something solid instead of sucking milk.

When my stomach was full, I lifted my head from the bowl and looked around me.

Everything was wonderfully moist and full of smells. The grass was succulent. The earth underneath it was rich and dark. I scratched up a little and stuck my nose right into it. Then I sneezed and shook my head to get the dirt off. I trotted over to the dalmatian's cage, and her brand-new puppies staggered over to their door to touch noses with me, just as I had touched noses with the terrier puppies not long ago.

After I greeted the younger dogs, I stepped away and lifted my nose higher. Even the air smelt full of possibilities. I smelt a lot of water, somewhere, more than I'd ever seen or smelt in a bowl. I smelt other dogs, and different animals, too: a squirrel that chattered on top of the fence, another animal – bigger, heavier, smellier – that had passed by outside the fence a few nights ago.

The man walked by me and opened the door of our cage to let my mother out. My brothers and sisters all rushed over to her, but I'd found a dead worm beneath my feet, and for the moment that was much more interesting.

The man left again, banging the gate shut behind him.

The gate . . .

My gaze focused on the doorknob.

There was a wooden table along the fence next to the gate, with a stool in front of it. I trotted over. The stool was low enough for me to claw my way up on to it. From there, it was only a quick jump-and-scramble to the top of the table.

There were empty food bowls on the table and a bag that smelt quite interesting. If my stomach had not been full, I might have been content to chew that bag open and munch on whatever was inside. But for the moment I had another interest.

I remembered how the man had put his hand on the metal doorknob, turned it, and pushed. Then the gate had opened.

Could I do something like that?

The doorknob was not round; it was a thin strip of metal. My tiny teeth were not much use for getting a grip on the thing, but I did my best. I bit hard and tugged and twisted my neck. Nothing happened except that I lost my balance and tumbled to the ground.

I sat up and barked at the gate in frustration. That didn't help either. My brothers and sisters raced over to jump on me, but I turned away from them. I wasn't in the mood to play.

I had something important to do.

I tried again, clambering on to the table and grabbing the knob with my teeth. This time I put my front paws up on the handle to keep myself from falling down, and to my surprise, the handle fell away beneath me. I slipped, and my whole body hit the lever on my way down. I thumped to the grass and looked up in surprise.

The gate was open!

Not very wide, certainly, but when I shoved my nose into the gap and pushed, it swung wider. I was free!

Eagerly, I trotted out, my little legs tripping over

themselves. A path lay right before me, two thin, parallel tracks worn into the dirt. This must be the way I should go.

But I turned back and looked at the gate. My mother was sitting just inside the open door, watching me.

She wouldn't be coming with me, I realized. She was going to stay inside the yard. I was on my own.

I thought about running back to her, snuggling into her warm side, getting a lick from her strong tongue. But I didn't.

Somehow I knew that puppies were meant to leave their mothers. It might be sad for both of them, but it was the way things were supposed to be. If I didn't leave her now, the man would come and carry me away from her, just as he had done to the terrier puppies.

And anyway, I knew deep inside that there was something on this side of the gate that I was meant to find. Or someone. There were other people in the world, I felt sure, and they would not all be like the man who'd fed us and opened our cage.

Somewhere in the world there were kind hands and gentle voices. And it was my job to hunt them out.

I set out in the world to do what I was supposed to do.

2

The dirt track under my feet was incredible! It smelt of rubber tyres, and of all the animals who had crossed it, and of damp rain from a few nights ago. I trotted along it happily, my short tail wagging. I snapped at a dragonfly that whizzed in front of me. I tromped through a puddle. I found a fantastic stick and dragged it with me until my neck started to hurt. Then I dropped it and dashed forward because I'd smelt something new. An empty cup! No, not empty. There was something sticky and sweet left inside it. I licked it carefully clean. Then I kept going.

After a while, the dirt track led me to a road of stuff that was as hard underfoot as the concrete inside my cage. I sniffed it and patted it gingerly with one paw. Then I decided to follow it, mostly because by doing that I'd head straight into the wind, which was bringing me wonderful new smells every second. Damp, rotting leaves! Trees! Pools of water! Squirrels! Mice! Worms!

Full of excitement, I set off on my adventure, but stopped. Something was quivering in a clump of leaves ahead of me.

Carefully, I stalked the moving thing, creeping closer and closer. Then whatever it was exploded right out of the leaves and buzzed straight at my face! A bug! I'd never seen one like that before. I jumped back and barked at it, to let it know I wasn't food. It turned and flew along the road, and I chased it. I'd show that bug who was the boss!

I heard the truck behind me, but I didn't stop until the bug flew straight up into a tree. Not fair! I barked in frustration. Then I realized that I couldn't hear the truck's growly engine behind me any more.

A door slammed. I turned. The truck had stopped by the edge of the road, and a man with wrinkled tan skin and muddy clothes got out. He knelt down and held out his hands.

'Hey, there, little fella!' he called.

I looked at him uncertainly. What kind of a person was this? What would those hands be like? Would they push me aside, like the first man I had known? Or would they be patient and gentle?

'You lost, fella? You lost?'

I wasn't sure about the hands yet, but the voice was kind. And he was talking right to me. The first man had never done that. And he'd never knelt down so that he was close to my level, either.

This man seemed OK. I trotted over to him.

He picked me up in hands large enough to reach all the way around me. And those hands *were* gentle. I was relieved, even when he lifted me up over his head for a moment. I didn't care for that, but he lowered me almost at once and held me cradled against his chest. He smelt of smoke and mud and sweat and the outdoors. It was delicious.

'You're a pretty little fella. You look like a purebred retriever. Where did you come from, fella?'

I licked the man's chin, which was rough with whiskers. He laughed.

Yes, I decided. *My name could be Fella.* I could stay with this man. I could be his dog, do what he told me, go where he went. That was what I was supposed to do, wasn't it? Stay with a person? I was pretty sure that was true. It felt right.

The man took me over to his truck and plopped me in the front seat. He climbed in next to me. I liked this! I liked it even better when he started the car and amazing new scents came pouring in through the window, open just a crack at the top.

I tried to put my front legs up on the window and get my nose as close as I could to that cool rush of air. It was fun, even though I toppled over every time the car hit a bump or made a turn. The man laughed and reached over to steady me with that warm, big, gentle hand.

Then he made a sharp turn that dumped me on the floor of the truck. That was OK. It smelt interesting down there, too. The truck screeched to a stop, and the man looked over at me.

'We're in the shade here,' he told me. I propped my feet up on the seat of the truck and looked at him. Then I hopped up and looked out the window. We were next to a building with several doors. The man nodded at one of the doors, next to a dark window.

'I'll only be a few minutes,' he told me, rolling up the windows. 'You'll be fine.'

I didn't realize he was leaving until he got out and shut the door behind him. Hey, wait a minute! What about me? Wasn't I his dog now? Wasn't I supposed to go wherever he did?

I watched the man go inside the building, and then I plopped myself down on the seat to wait. I found a cloth strap and chewed on it for a while, but it wasn't very tasty. Bored, I settled down for a nap. The sun had shifted and was now coming in through the window, nice and warm on my back.

When I awoke, the sun was more than warm. It was *hot*.

The air in the truck was damp and tasted stale. I started panting. Then I started whimpering. I put my paws up on the window so I could see if the man was coming back. No sign of him! And the glass in the window was hot enough to burn against my paws. I dropped back down to the seat, pacing back and forth. The panting wasn't doing much good. I wasn't getting any cooler.

Everything inside the car seemed to be getting blurry and fuzzy around the edges. I lay down on the seat, thinking of the bowls of water the man used to bring us, of the puddle on the dirt track, of cool, fresh smells on the breeze.

My tongue was hanging out until it touched the cloth seat, but each gulp of hot air inside my mouth only made things worse. My whole body began to tremble.

I couldn't get up to peer out of the window again. All I could do was lift my eyes to the glass.

There was a face staring in! I couldn't see it clearly, and I couldn't smell it at all. But surely it was the man. He would open a door. He would get me out!

The face vanished.

I slumped with disappointment, feeling so heavy

that it seemed I could sink into the soft cloth of the seat. My paws were starting to twitch all by themselves.

Then there was a stupendous crash. The whole truck rocked on its wheels. A stone bounced into the seat next to me, and clear, shiny pebbles scattered over my back. I lifted my head, and a cool kiss of air swept through the broken window and over my face.

Hands slid around me. They were not the hands of the man; they were smaller, and smoother, and even more gentle. I couldn't move as I was lifted towards a worried face framed by long black hair. A woman's face.

'You poor puppy. You poor, poor puppy,' she whispered.

My name is Fella, I thought to myself.

The next thing I knew, I was lying on soft grass while cool, clear water trickled all over me, from my nose to my tail. The woman stood over me, holding a plastic jug. Nothing had ever felt so good.

I shuddered with pleasure and lifted my mouth to lap and bite at the sweet stream.

'That's right, puppy. That's right,' the woman encouraged me.

A man stood nearby – not the one who had left me

in the truck. A different man. He was watching me closely.

'Do you think he'll be OK?' the woman asked.

'Looks like the water is doing the job,' he answered.

I felt worry from both of them, and affection, and care. These were the kind of people I had set out into the world to find. I rolled over on my back so that the water would wash over my hot tummy, and the woman laughed.

'Such a cute puppy!' she said. 'Do you know what kind it is?'

'Looks like a golden retriever,' the man answered. 'And, uh, he's a boy.'

'Oh, puppy,' the woman murmured.

Yes, I could be Puppy; I could be Fella; I could be whatever they wanted. When the woman swept me up in her arms, not even caring about the big wet splat my soaking fur made on her blouse, I kissed her face until she closed her eyes and giggled.

'You're coming home with me, little guy,' she told me. 'I've got someone I want you to meet.'

She took me away from the truck and into a car, holding me on her lap while she drove. I leaned into her, sniffing. She smelt clean, like soap, and sweet, like flowers, and there was an animal odour on her clothes, one I'd never smelt before. Now and then she took a hand down from the steering wheel to stroke me. Very nice.

She stopped the car once and left me inside, which made me pace and whimper, but she left a window open an inch or so, and in a moment she was back. I cuddled up on her lap again while she drove, until, feeling better, I heaved myself off to explore. Two streams of clean, cold air flowed out of some vents into my face, and I sniffed them and shook my head, sending water splattering off my ears. The woman laughed.

The cold air on my wet fur was actually beginning to make me shiver, so I climbed down to the floor, where it was a little warmer. There was a carpet down there, soft and rough at the same time, and I was ready to curl up for another little nap.

I woke up when the car stopped. The woman reached down with those soft hands and picked me up. I blinked sleepily at her.

'Oh, you are so cute,' she whispered. As she held me against her chest, I could feel her heart beat. She was excited. I yawned and shook off the last traces of my nap. After she let me down, I squatted and peed in the grass. Then I was ready to face whatever had this nice woman so worked up.

'Ethan!' she called. 'Come here! I want you to meet someone.'

I looked up at her curiously. We were in front of a big white house. I wondered what I'd find here. Would there be cages? Other dogs? A big yard with a wooden fence?

The front door of the house banged open and a human being came racing out. A new kind of human being. I'd never seen one like this before.

He jumped down the cement steps and landed on the grass. His hair was dark like the woman's, but cut short, above his ears. He was smaller than she was. His head didn't come up to her shoulder.

He stared at me. I stared back. He was, I realized, a young human. A child. A male one. His mouth broke into a huge grin and he spread out his arms.

'A puppy!' he sang.

We ran to each other. He flopped down to pick me up, and I could not stop licking him. He could not stop giggling. We rolled together in the grass.

I hadn't known that there was such a thing as a boy in the world. But now that I'd found one, I was sure that there could not be anything better. He smelt fascinating, of sweat and soap and mud and something meaty that he'd been eating, and also of the same animal I'd smelt on the woman's clothes. I burrowed my nose into his hair and under the collar of his shirt and sniffed and sniffed.

A boy! I think this was what I had been looking for when I stepped out of that yard. A boy like this.

3

By the end of that first day I would come to know the boy very well, not just by smell but also by the way he looked, the way he sounded, the way he moved. He had light eyes to go with that black hair. He had a way of turning his head to look at me as if he were trying to do more than see me – to learn me by heart. And his voice bubbled with joy whenever he talked to me.

But for now I was drinking in his scent, burrowing into his shirt, licking the taste of whatever he'd eaten off his fingers.

'Can we keep him, Mum? Can we keep him?' the boy gasped between giggles.

The woman squatted down to pat my head. 'Well,

you know your dad, Ethan. He's going to want to hear that you'll take care of him—'

'I will! I will!'

'And that you'll walk him and feed him—'

'Every day! I'll walk him and feed him and brush him and give him water—'

'And you'll have to clean up when he poops in the yard.'

Ethan didn't answer that one.

'I bought some puppy food at the store. Let's give him some dinner. You won't believe what happened. I had to run to the petrol station and get a jug of water. The poor thing was nearly dead with heat exhaustion,' the woman said.

Ethan wasn't really listening. 'Want some dinner? Huh? Dinner?' he asked, sticking his face close to mine.

Sounded pretty good to me.

Then something incredible happened. The boy picked me up and carried me right into the house! I'd never even imagined that might be possible. Did it mean that I wouldn't be living in a wire cage with a concrete floor? That I could stay where the people stayed?

I was going to like it here just fine.

Some of the floors were soft, and sunk into that softness was the same animal odour I'd smelt on the woman and the boy. Other floors were slick and hard. They made my feet skitter out from under me as I tried to follow the boy wherever he went.

When Ethan saw me struggling to walk, he picked me up. And the flow of love from him was so strong it gave me a hollow feeling in my tummy, almost like hunger. I leaned into him, lapping at his chin. I wanted him to know that I already felt the same way.

He put me down next to a bowl filled with something delicious. I pounced on it. It had been a long time since I'd last eaten, back in the yard with my brothers and sisters. Ethan refilled the bowl for me when I had emptied it, and he gave me water, too, and then he wrestled with me. He dangled a length of cloth by my nose, and when I snapped at it, he tugged. I tugged back and growled as fiercely as I could, which made the boy laugh so much he dropped the cloth. I shook it triumphantly. Mine! I'd won!

Then a vibration rumbled through the house, and I heard a loud slam. I knew that noise meant a car door had been shut.

'Your father's home,' said the woman, whose name was Mum.

Ethan stood up and faced the front door. Mum came and stood beside him. I gave the cloth a few more shakes, but it wasn't nearly as interesting without the boy attached to the other end.

The door opened. 'Hi, Dad!' Ethan yelled.

A man stepped in and stood looking back and forth from the boy to the woman. 'OK, what is it?' he asked.

I leaped forward to wrestle with the boy's shoelaces. The man's gaze dropped to me.

'Dad, Mum found this puppy . . .' Ethan began.

'He was locked in a car, nearly dead from heatstroke,' Mum said.

'Can we keep him, Dad?'

I yanked hard on a shoelace. It fought back.

'Oh, I don't know,' the man said, shaking his head. 'Do you know how much work a puppy is? You're only eight years old, Ethan. It's too much responsibility.'

I pulled even harder, and I felt the shoelace give. I tried to run away with it, but somehow it was still attached to the boy's foot, so that it yanked me back, tumbling me head over heels. Snarling, I dived once more on to the boy's feet, biting the lace again, giving it a furious shake.

'I'll take care of him, and I'll walk him and feed him and wash him,' Ethan was saying. 'He's the best puppy in the world, Dad! He's already house-trained!'

The shoelace had given up and just flopped limply in my mouth. Since I'd shown the shoelace who was boss, I decided this would be a good time to take a little break. I squatted, leaving a brown blob on top of a wet stain on the carpet.

Suddenly, the people got very busy.

After they finished whatever it was they were doing with wet cloths and squares of soft paper and some kind of spray that smelt so sharp it made my eyes water, the boy picked me up again. He sat down on the floor with me on his lap, leaning against a chair.

Mum and Dad sat nearby.

'George?' Mum said.

'George?' Ethan said. 'Here, George! Hi, George!'

'Skippy?' Dad said.

'Skippy!' Ethan said. 'Are you Skippy? Here, Skippy!'

It got exhausting. I plopped down for a nap with my head on the boy's leg.

When I woke up, the people still hadn't got tired of this game. But at least Ethan took me out into the backyard to play. There was lots of good grass and tasty sticks and buried acorns and fallen leaves. And of course, the boy, who was the best plaything of all.

'Here, Bailey! Here, Bailey!' Ethan called, slapping his knees.

Of course I hurried to him; why wouldn't I want to be near the boy? He ran away, and I chased him around and around in a huge circle. 'Bailey! Bailey!' the boy shouted. 'He's Bailey!'

I'd be Bailey, sure. If that was what the boy wanted, I was happy to be Bailey forever.

I stayed very close to Ethan for the next few days, while I was getting used to all of the things about my new home. It certainly was different from life in the cage with my mother and littermates. For one thing, there was that strange animal I'd smelt on the boy's clothes, and on Mum's, and on the carpets that covered the floor.

'Bailey, I want you to meet Smokey the cat,' Ethan said not long after I'd got my new name.

He carried me back inside the house, and, holding me tightly against his chest, he turned so that I could see an animal not much bigger than I was, sitting in the middle of the floor. He was covered in brown-and-grey fur and had tiny ears that looked like they'd be fun to bite. His eyes grew wide and dark when he spotted me.

So this was a cat, was it?

I struggled to get down to play with this new friend, but Ethan held me tight.

'Smokey, this is Bailey,' he said.

Slowly, he bent over to place me on the floor. I ran to Smokey. This new home not only had a boy, it had something furry and my size to chase and wrestle with!

Things just could not get better!

My tongue was out to give my new friend a greeting, but he pulled back his lips to show a set of teeth that were tiny but deadly sharp. Then he arched his back so that suddenly he looked a lot bigger. He let out a loud, sharp hiss. That didn't look friendly at all!

But at the same time, he was wagging his tail. I skidded to a stop, puzzled. Did this cat want to play or not?

That tail puffed up wide as every single hair on it stiffened, and Smokey stopped wagging it and let it rise slowly straight up in the air. I tried to inch in and give him a friendly sniff right under the tail, to show him I meant no harm. But he must not have got the message, because he jumped away and spat at me, lifting a paw with very sharp claws spread wide.

'Aw, Smokey, be a nice cat. Be a nice cat,' Ethan coaxed.

Smokey glared at Ethan. I gave his face a warm lick, still trying to be as friendly as I could, but all I got back was a bat on the nose from those sharp claws.

OK, well, that was that. I was more than ready to play with Smokey whenever he wanted, but I had more important things to worry about than a snotty cat. I had a new family to get to know and a new home to explore.

The boy lived in a small room full of wonderful toys, very good for chewing. Mum and Dad shared a room that had no toys at all. One small white room had a big bowl of water I could drink from, if I climbed into it. There weren't any toys there, either, unless you counted the roll of thin paper mounted on a wall. Once I got my teeth in some of that, I could pull it off in one long train that wound around me and followed me through the halls. That was fun, at least the first few times.

But I liked other rooms better, especially the one that smelt like food. I couldn't get *at* the food, though, which was frustrating. It was all locked up behind doors that I didn't know how to open.

Each time I needed to squat and relieve myself, everybody in my new family went crazy, scooping me up and racing out the door with me, plopping me down in the grass and watching me carefully until I'd recovered from the shock and could go about my business. When I did, they'd praise me so much that I wondered if this was why they'd brought me home. It seemed like what they were most interested in.

The bizarre thing was, though, that if I did *the very same thing* on the carpets inside the house, nobody praised me at all! And if I squatted on some papers that they'd put down on the floor for me to rip up, I'd get a bit of praise – but not too much.

It was all very bewildering.

'No!' Mum or Ethan would shout when I wet the

floor. 'Good boy!' they'd sing when I peed in the grass. 'OK, that's good,' they'd say when I left a puddle on the papers. I could not understand what in the world was wrong with them.

Mum laughed at me when I wrestled with Ethan's socks, and she bent down to rub my ears when I fell asleep in a patch of sunlight. Dad didn't pay me much attention, although he did seem to like it when I got up early in the morning to watch him eat breakfast. Of course I kept a sharp eye out for any scraps of scrambled egg or crumbs of toast that might drift down to the floor.

But neither of them loved me like Ethan did. I felt adoration flow out of Ethan whenever he was near me.

And that made sense, after all. Ethan was my boy.

4

Sometimes Dad and Ethan would sit together at a table in the evenings, talking quietly while the smell of something strange and sharp and eye-watering filled the air. Dad would let me lie on his feet. That was nice, since Ethan's feet didn't reach the floor.

'Look, Bailey, we built an aeroplane,' the boy said after one of these sessions, thrusting a toy near my nose. I had to blink and back up a bit from the smell, so I didn't try to take it or chew it. Making noises that sounded like the car when it went fast – 'Vroom, vroom!' – the boy raced around the house holding the toy. I helped by chasing him.

Later he put the toy up on a shelf with others that

smelt the same, and that was the end of that, until he and Dad decided to build another one.

'This one is a rocket, Bailey,' Ethan told me, showing me a toy shaped like a stick. But what use was a stick-like thing that smelt too bad to chew? I turned my nose away. 'We're going to land one on the moon one day, and then people will live there, too. Do you want to be a space dog?'

I heard the word 'dog', and it sounded as if there was a question, so I wagged. *Yes,* I thought. *I would be happy to clean the plates, if that's what you're asking.*

Clean the Plates was a game where the boy put a sticky plate on the floor, and I licked it until it was shiny. It was one of my jobs, but only when Mum wasn't watching.

Mostly, though, my job was to stay near the boy. When it grew dark at night, he would carry me up to his room, since the stairs were too steep for my short legs. There was a box there with a soft pillow, and he'd put me into it.

I understood that I was supposed to stay there until Mum and Dad came in and said goodnight. Then the boy would call softly to me and I'd scramble, with his help, up on to the bed. We'd curl up together. If I woke up in the middle of the night and got bored, I could always chew on the boy.

During the day, Ethan and I often played in the

backyard, where there was lots of room for the best wrestling and chasing games. And then one day, Ethan clipped a long rope on to my collar and introduced me to an entirely new place – 'the neighbourhood'.

Ethan ran down the pavement, with me right at his heels, and soon we were surrounded by a bunch of other girls and boys, some bigger than Ethan, some smaller, all of them with their hands out, eager to stroke me.

I was happy to oblige. I leaned into their hands and lapped at their fingers and listened to their giggles.

'This is my dog, Bailey,' Ethan said proudly. He scooped me up, and I wiggled at the sound of my name. 'Look, Chelsea,' he said, offering me to a girl his size. 'He's a golden retriever. My mother rescued him. He was dying in a car from heat exhaustion. When he gets old enough, I'm going to take him to my grandparents' farm.'

Chelsea cuddled me to her chest and gazed into my eyes. Her hair was long and even lighter than mine, and she smelt quite interesting, of sugar and milk and flowers and another dog. 'You are sweet. You are so sweet, Bailey. I love you,' she sang to me.

I liked Chelsea. Whenever we were out in the neighbourhood and she saw me, she would drop to her knees and let me tug on her long blond hair. I soon learned that the dog scent on her clothes came from Marshmallow, a long-haired brown-and-white dog, older than I was. When Chelsea let Marshmallow out of her yard, we would wrestle for hours, and sometimes Ethan would join us, playing, playing, playing.

'Bailey!' Ethan would laugh when I got hold of his shirt and tugged. 'Here, Bailey,' he would call, and I'd come running to throw myself on top of him. 'Bailey, Bailey, Bailey,' he would whisper in my ear at night.

I loved my name, because of how the boy said it. Whenever he used it, I came to him. That was how I learned my first trick – Come.

Ethan would call, 'Bailey!' and as I trotted towards him, he'd add, 'Come!' Then he'd feed me a treat. Excellent! Pretty soon I learned that I was supposed to head for anybody who said 'Come', even Mum or Dad.

There were other tricks, too. 'Sit, Bailey, sit!' Ethan would say. He would climb on top of me, forcing my rear end down to the ground. Then he'd let me have a dog biscuit. That wasn't quite as much fun as Come, but since the boy liked it, I put up with it.

Dog Door was another game Ethan liked to play. We'd go out in the garage, a large, bare room that smelt of metal and dirty air and tasty rubbish and a sharp scent that I had learned was called petrol. In the garage, there was a door with a plastic flap in it that led out to the backyard. 'Dog Door!' Ethan would call, and then he'd shove me through the flap and out on to the grass. When I'd stick my nose back through the flap, I'd get my biscuit.

A day came when we played Dog Door a lot. That night, I realized that my legs had grown long enough for me to hop up on Ethan's bed all by myself. That was a good thing, because the nights were starting to get cooler. I liked the fact that, anytime I wanted, I could get up on that bed and curl up right next to my boy's warmth.

The boy loved me. I loved him. From the second we woke up until the moment we fell asleep, we were together.

And then everything changed.

The morning after the day we had played Dog Door so much, the boy was up early, not long after sunrise. Mum was running in and out of various rooms. Everybody seemed excited. I stayed right at Ethan's heels, excited, too. What were we going to be doing together?

'Take care of Bailey!' Mum called at one point. Smokey the cat glanced down at me from where he was sitting on the counter. It was so unfair that he could get up there where all the good food smells were, and I couldn't. I gave my new chew toy a good shake just to show him that I didn't care.

'Bailey!' the boy called out, and I heard a funny thumping noise. So I went to investigate. He was dragging my dog bed down the stairs. Why was he doing that? Did he need my help? He carried the bed out to the garage, and I followed him.

'Dog door,' the boy said to me.

I sniffed his pockets. I couldn't smell any biscuits. What would be the point of playing Dog Door without biscuits? I turned away and started to lift my leg on a bicycle instead.

'Bailey!' There was impatience in the boy's voice, and I remembered how funny all the people in my family seemed to get about perfectly normal things like marking territory with a little urine. I lowered my leg and turned to look at him.

'You sleep here, OK, Bailey?' Ethan said. 'You be a good dog. If you need to go to the toilet, you go out the dog door, OK? Dog door, Bailey. I have to go to school now. OK? I love you, Bailey.'

Ethan gave me a hug and a good scratch under the collar. I licked his ear and his nose. When he headed back inside the house, of course I followed him. But at the door that led into the kitchen, he stopped and shook his head.

'No, Bailey, you stay in the garage until I get home. Dog door, OK, Bailey? You be a good dog.'

And he shut the door in my face!

My boy actually did that! He walked through the door and shut it, so that I was on one side of it and he was on the other. And what were all those words he'd said to me? 'Stay'? 'Dog door'? 'Good dog'? How were those connected? Was there something he wanted me to do so that he could give me a biscuit? Which one was Stay, again?

And where had my boy gone? Why would he go anywhere without me?

None of this made any sense at all! I sniffed around the garage. The smells were interesting, different from the ones inside the house, but I wasn't in the mood to explore. I wanted my boy! I barked. The door to the house stayed shut tight. I scratched it. Still nothing.

I heard some children yelling from the front of the house and ran to the big garage door, hoping it would lift up. Sometimes it did that, and then Dad or Mum drove a car in or out. But that didn't happen this time. The big door stayed firmly down.

A loud truck of some kind swept up the voices of the children and carried them away. A few minutes later I heard Mum's car drive off. And then the world, which had been so full of life and fun and noise, became quiet. Horribly quiet.

I barked for a while. Surely someone would hear me and realize that I had been shut in the garage and come to get me out!

Nobody did, though. My barking didn't make anything happen at all.

I sniffed around the door to the house. I could smell Smokey on the other side of it, and I was sure he was happy that he was there and I was here.

I scratched the door. I chewed on some old shoes I found in a corner. I ripped up my dog bed. I found a black plastic bag, tied shut, full of clothing. I got my teeth into that, too, ripped it open, and scattered the clothes around the garage. I peed in one corner and pooped in another. I tipped over a big metal container that smelt wonderful, and inside it I found a few pieces of chicken and some spaghetti and half a waffle. I took care of all that, and I licked out a can of fish that smelt like Smokey's breath. I ate some paper. I knocked over my water dish and chewed on it.

There was nothing to do.

When were the people coming back? Where was my boy? Now that I'd found the boy and figured out that my job was to be near him, how could he go away and leave me? When I'd got myself out of the big yard and gone into the world, looking for what I needed, I'd never imagined this.

Would I be alone forever?

5

After the longest day of my entire life, I heard Mum's car pull into the driveway. Her car door slammed, and I heard running feet pound through the house.

'Bailey!' the boy shouted, and the door to the garage flew open.

I tackled Ethan, overjoyed. He was back! He'd come to save me! We fell on to the floor of the kitchen together. But he pushed me away while I was busy licking his face and snuffling up all the unfamiliar smells on his clothing. He got to his feet again and looked into the garage.

'Oh, Bailey,' he said, sounding sad.

Why on earth was he sad when we were finally together again? It was so exciting! I tore past him and skittered into the house, leaping over the furniture. I spotted Smokey and chased him up the stairs, barking when he dived under Mum and Dad's bed. I dashed back down the stairs to Ethan again, my tail beating the air.

Mum was standing next to Ethan now, and they were both looking through the door into the garage.

'Bailey! Quiet down!' Mum called sternly.

'Bad dog, Bailey,' the boy said crossly.

I was astounded. Bad dog? *Me?* They had accidentally locked me in the garage and forgotten about me and left me there *all day,* but I was willing to forgive them. Why were they scowling like that and shaking their fingers at *me?*

Moments later I was back in the garage, helping the boy as he picked up everything I'd played with and put most of it into the tall metal bin that I had knocked over. Mum came out and picked up the clothes, sorting through them, putting some into the bin and taking some back inside the house. But no one praised me for finding out where those clothes had been hiding.

Why were they in such grumpy moods? I couldn't be grumpy at all. I stayed close to Ethan and kept my tail flashing back and forth. I gave him a lick whenever I could.

'Dog door,' the boy said crossly. But he seemed to have forgotten how to play the game, because he didn't push me out and he didn't give me any treats. I was beginning to think that 'dog door' meant the same thing as 'bad dog'. What a disappointment! I was quite sure I hadn't been a bad dog at all. I hoped Mum and Ethan would cheer up soon.

It had been a very upsetting day, but I was willing to put the whole thing behind me. It seemed that the humans didn't feel the same way, though, because as soon as Dad came home, there was a lot of talking and even a little yelling, and I could feel that Dad was angry at me. I snuck into the living room to stay out of his way. Smokey sat on a windowsill and sneered at me.

Dad and the boy left right after dinner. Mum sat at the table and stared at papers. She didn't move even when I came up to her and put a nice wet ball right in her lap, inviting her to play. 'Oh, yuck, Bailey,' she said.

When the boy and Dad came home, Ethan called me into the garage and showed me a big wooden box. I sniffed it, smelling new wood and fresh paint. Not my favourite smells.

It seemed that Ethan had come up with a new trick to show me. 'Doghouse!' he called, and he climbed inside the house. Of course I climbed in right after him. There was a thin pad on the floor for us to lie on. The space was hot and tight with the two of us in there, but I didn't really mind. I'd been apart from my boy so long; it was good to be close to him now. I licked his hair.

'Doghouse, Bailey. This is your doghouse,' he said.

Then he crawled back out and got some dog biscuits, which of course made the whole game even better. 'Doghouse' apparently meant 'crawl into the doghouse with Ethan and eat a biscuit.' We practised Dog Door, too, properly this time, with Ethan pushing on my rear end until I went through the door and handing me a biscuit afterwards.

While we did all this, Dad moved around the garage, putting things up on high shelves and tying a rope over the top of the big metal container.

When the boy got tired of tricks, we went inside and wrestled for a while. 'Time for bed,' Mum said.

'Oh, Mum, please? Can I stay up?'

'We both have school tomorrow, Ethan. Time for you to say goodnight to Bailey.'

Mum and Dad and Ethan were always making words like this at each other, and I rarely paid too much attention. This time I did lift up my head when I heard my name. All of a sudden, the boy seemed sad. His shoulders slumped.

'OK, Bailey,' he said, but there was no happiness in his voice. I looked up at him and tilted my head, puzzled. 'Time for bed.'

I trotted over to the foot of the stairs. But for some reason, Ethan walked over to the garage door. Maybe he wanted to play Doghouse once more before we settled down? That was OK with me, as long as there'd be a biscuit involved.

Once I'd followed Ethan out into the garage, I figured I'd been right. 'Doghouse,' he said, but his voice was glum. I walked over to the doghouse and then paused and looked back at Ethan. Wasn't he getting in with me? Had he forgotten how to play?

Ethan actually walked back inside the house and shut the door on me *again*!

I barked, trying to get his attention, trying to make him see he'd made another mistake. Or *was* it a mistake? Did they really think I'd been a bad dog? They couldn't! Was it because I'd peed and pooped in the garage? But no one had been here to let me out! Was it because I'd chewed up my dog bed? But I never slept in the thing, anyway. It was just for show.

Did they really expect me to stay out here in the garage all night long? *By myself?*

It couldn't be!

I couldn't stand the thought of the boy lying in bed without me, all alone. The idea was so sad it made me want to chew shoes.

I began to whimper. Softly at first, and then louder. And louder. Surely someone in the family would hear me. They'd understand that I needed to be with my boy!

A long time went by. No one came.

My cries grew louder.

After forever, the door to the house eased open a crack. 'Bailey,' the boy whispered. 'Shhh, Bailey, it's OK.'

I almost barked with relief, but I got the sense from Ethan that I shouldn't. I kept quiet, but I nuzzled and licked his knees and legs frantically as he slipped through the door, carrying a blanket and a pillow. 'OK, doghouse, doghouse,' he told me in a low voice. And we were playing the right way now, because he crawled in, too. I crammed in after him. I didn't even care that he didn't have a biscuit.

Ethan wiggled around until he had half the blanket underneath him and half over his legs. It was certainly snug in there; the boy's feet stuck out of the door, and my back legs did, too. I didn't care. It meant I was closer to my boy. With a sigh, I put my head on his chest. He stroked my ears.

'Good dog, Bailey,' he murmured.

So that strange and bewildering day had a nice ending after all. I closed my eyes, and the boy and I went to sleep together.

A little while later, I was woken up by a quiet click coming from the door to the house. It was the sound of the latch opening. I opened my eyes and peered out of the doghouse to see Mum and Dad standing in the rectangle of light that led into the kitchen. I wagged my tail softly a few times to greet them, but I didn't move my head. I didn't want to wake up the boy.

Finally, Dad came out. Gently, he tugged Ethan and the blanket out of the doghouse. Naturally, I came, too. Ethan stirred a little and then slumped back into sleep as his father picked him up.

Mum gestured to me. 'Shh, Bailey,' she whispered. Dad carried Ethan up to bed, and Mum and I followed. No one tried to stop me as I hopped right up on the bed with Ethan.

I settled down with Ethan's chest for a pillow. Without opening his eyes, he put a sleepy arm around me.

6

But the next day, as if nobody had learned anything, I was back out in the garage *again*! What was the matter with these people?

This time there was far less to do. I did manage to get the pad off the floor of the doghouse and shred it up pretty well. I knocked over the metal bin, but I couldn't get the lid off. Too bad; I could smell some scraps of last night's macaroni and cheese in there.

There was nothing on the floor of the garage that I could chew. I couldn't reach the stuff that Dad had put on the shelves last night.

This was no fun at all.

Restlessly, I wandered over to the dog door and

scratched at it. The flap moved and a waft of damp, delicious air from the backyard drifted in. It had rained in the night, and I loved the way the water clung to the air and dripped from the leaves of the trees, scattering down in showers when a breeze came by. Damp air carried so many more smells than dry. My nose picked up exhaust from cars, Mum's roses, burnt toast from next door, wet earth, living leaves on the trees and dead ones scattered on the ground.

I leaned against the dog door, my nose working hard to draw the smells in. I leaned further. And then, suddenly, I was out in the yard! The boy hadn't even pushed me!

I tore around the backyard, barking with excitement. I was out! I was outside, surrounded by all of those marvellous smells!

I squatted and peed into the grass. It was nicer to do it outside, anyway, even apart from the fuss that all the humans made about their floors and rugs. I liked to wipe my paws on the lawn after I went, so that the scent from the sweat on my pads ended up on the blades of grass. And it was just more satisfying, somehow, to lift my leg and mark the corners of the yard instead of a leg of the couch.

I raced around the yard some more, my nose up in the wind, picking up whatever smells the breeze bought me. Being in the yard alone was not as much fun as being there with the boy, but it was definitely better than the garage!

However, when the breeze brought new, cold raindrops my way, I began to think that the garage had its good points. I went back to the dog door and poked my nose at it. If I'd got *out* on my own, was there a chance that . . .

Yes! I could get *back* into the garage all by myself, too! Under a roof once more, I shook a little water from my fur and wished the boy were here to see what I had learned. I was sure he'd call me a good dog. There would probably be a biscuit in it for me.

After the rain ended, I tried my new trick with the dog door again, and sure enough, I was out in the backyard for a second time. I dug a hole, chewed the hose, and barked at Smokey, who was sitting in a window and pretending not to notice me. When a large yellow bus pulled up in front of the house, Ethan and several more neighbourhood kids, including Chelsea, tumbled out. I jumped up to put my paws against the fence, and the boy ran to me, laughing.

The doghouse didn't get much use after that. But every now and then, Ethan and I still played Doghouse. It would usually happen when he got off the bus with his shoulders slumped, smelling tired and sad. Then he'd crawl inside the doghouse and call me, and I'd push myself in, too. It got a little harder to get in there as months went by, and I had to leave more and more of my rear end outside. But I did it, because the boy wanted me.

He would put his arm around me and tell me things quietly. 'Nobody would play with me at break-time, Bailey,' he'd whisper. Or, 'I can't believe my teacher gave me a D. I worked so hard on that project, Bailey. It's not fair.' Or sometimes he'd just tell me, 'You're lucky to be a dog, Bailey. It's tough being a boy.'

I didn't understand most of the words, although I wagged every time he said my name. But I knew that he was sad, and that being with me in the doghouse made him feel better. I would sit perfectly still with him, however long he needed me. This was my job, I came to understand, and it was even more important than staying close to the boy, or playing with the boy, or learning tricks with the boy, or sleeping beside the boy at night. I was supposed to comfort Ethan whenever he needed me.

Each time Ethan and I went out to play in the neighbourhood, a crowd of kids would show up. I got to know most of them. There was Billy, who usually smelt like peanut butter, and Chelsea, of course, who'd bring Marshmallow with her. And now and then there'd be a new kid with a new smell for me to memorize.

So when Todd arrived, I figured it was good news. First, it meant that Mum baked delicious cookies for Ethan to take over to the new family, and she gave me a few as a reward for keeping her company in the kitchen. Second, a new boy to play with was always fun.

Todd was the same age as Ethan, and they began to spend a lot of time together. Todd had a little sister named Linda, but he wouldn't let her play with them most of the time. I didn't know why. I liked her fine. She fed me sugary treats when nobody was watching.

There was a game that Todd liked to play, down by a small creek that ran behind the houses. He'd bring a pack of matches and burn things – leaves, sticks, Linda's dolls. I stayed a little distance away, since I didn't like the way the matches smelt when Todd struck them. And the smell of Linda's plastic dolls when their hair lit up and their faces shrank and shrivelled was horrible.

Ethan didn't want to touch the matches, but he'd watch. He didn't laugh as much as Todd did, though.

One day, Todd announced that he had a firecracker this time. I had never seen anything like the brightly coloured stick he was holding, and I didn't like its smell – it was like the matches, only worse. It smouldered for a bit on the ground, and then there was a flash and a bang so loud that I leaped across the creek. Quickly, I ran back to the boy, barking.

Ethan patted my head. 'It's OK, Bailey. Easy, boy. It's just noise. Don't worry.'

I sniffed cautiously around on the ground where the stick had been. There were some scraps of paper and cardboard there now, and a piece of one of Linda's dolls. All of these things had a charred, smoky smell that I didn't like. Somehow it said 'danger' to me.

'Come on, Ethan. Get it!' Todd said impatiently while I sniffed.

Ethan hesitated. I lifted my nose from the ground.

'Come *on,*' Todd insisted, and Ethan turned towards his house. Of course, I followed.

Ethan went to his room and took something off a high shelf. I got a faint whiff of that same smell that came off the table when Dad and Ethan sat there together after dinner.

'No, not the rocket,' Ethan decided and put back the toy he was holding. He grabbed another one and ran outside to where Todd was waiting.

'Cool aeroplane!' Todd said.

There was excitement coming off Ethan, but it was a strange kind of excitement. I could smell something like fear in it, and I danced around nervously, barking a little, as Ethan and Todd fussed over the toy in Ethan's hands. I could smell the sharp flare of a match being lighted, and then Ethan threw his toy up into the air.

Bang!

Another noise! I shook my ears, which hurt from the loudness. Both boys were standing still, looking up into the sky, where smelly, charred bits of plastic were drifting down to the creek.

'Cool!' Todd yelled. Ethan said nothing. The excitement and the fear were both draining out of him, leaving something heavy and sad behind.

'Come on, Ethan, get another one!' Todd shouted. But Ethan shook his head. Todd lit more firecrackers and tossed them into the air, and I ran in circles as the noises went off.

Ethan picked up a bit of plastic from a rock near the creek bed, one a little smaller than his hand.

Behind Ethan's back, Todd looked at me and grinned. He tossed a firecracker in my direction.

Bang! The thing burst so close I felt the wind from the explosion whoosh against my fur. I yelped and ran to Ethan, who dropped the chunk of plastic to hug me.

'Come on, Bailey,' he said. 'Let's go home.'

The next day Ethan and I went to Chelsea's house after school. Marshmallow and I wrestled and ran in their backyard. I liked Marshmallow. She was always ready for a good game of Tug on a Stick or This Ball Is Mine.

Sometimes I even got to go and see Marshmallow on my own. Whenever Ethan went away on the school bus, leaving me alone in the backyard, I would check the gate. It didn't have a doorknob, like the gate to the first yard I'd lived in, so there was nothing I could bite or tug with my teeth. But sometimes, if I gave this gate a good hard shove with my paw or my nose, it would swing open. Then I'd take a stroll around the neighbourhood.

I'd visit Marshmallow, touching noses with her through the wire fence around her backyard, and I'd mark all of her trees carefully. After that I'd go wherever my nose took me, until I remembered that the boy might be waiting. That meant it was time to trot home.

One day I wandered further than usual, so that when I turned back it was just starting to get dark. I began to worry that I might have missed the time when Ethan was supposed to get off the bus. What would he do without me there to greet him?

I cut through the creek, which took me right past Todd's backyard. He was playing on the muddy bank, and when he saw me, he called out to me.

'Hey, Bailey. Here, Bailey.' He held out his hand.

I eyed him with suspicion. There was just something inside Todd that I didn't trust. And that something seemed to be stronger now that he was on his own, with no other humans nearby.

'Come on, boy,' he said, slapping his hand against his leg. He turned and walked towards his house.

What could I do? Come was one of the tricks Ethan had taught me. I knew that it meant I was supposed to follow the person who said it.

I lowered my head and trailed after Todd into his house.

7

Todd let me in through the back door into a kitchen. He eased the door shut behind us without a sound. Curtains were pulled over the windows, and the room had a dark, gloomy feel and a stale, chilly smell. I usually love the way kitchens smell, but not this one.

Todd whispered, 'Come on, Bailey!' and I followed him out of the kitchen and down a hallway. About halfway along it we passed a doorway to a living room, where a woman was slumped on a couch, watching television. She didn't move or even turn her head as we went past.

But someone else moved. After we were past the door, Todd turned back. I paused, too. He scowled as a small figure came to the doorway that led into the living room, outlined against the greyish, flickering light of the TV.

It was Linda, Todd's sister. She saw me and her eyes grew wider. She came forward.

'No,' Todd hissed at her.

I certainly knew *that* word. I cringed at the sharp tone of Todd's voice. Linda put a finger in her mouth, chewing at the nail, but she didn't back up. She held her other hand out to me. I licked it.

Todd stepped forward to push Linda away. 'Leave me alone,' he said sharply to her.

Then he opened a door, grabbed my collar, and pulled me inside. He didn't have to do that. I would have gone with him, even though I would rather have stayed with Linda. I knew what I was supposed to do to be a good dog.

Todd shut the door and I heard the lock make a clicking sound. I sniffed at piles of smelly clothes on the floor and found a plate under an old T-shirt with half a piece of toast on it. I quickly ate it. Clean the Plate was always my job when a plate was on the floor.

Then I checked on what Todd was doing. He was walking quickly around the room, his hands shoved into his pockets. 'OK,' he said. 'OK, now . . . now . . .'

He sat at his desk and opened a drawer. I could

smell firecrackers in there; the odour stung my nose. I didn't like it. I backed up to the other side of the room, under a window.

'I don't know where Bailey is,' Todd muttered. 'I haven't seen Bailey.'

I wagged at my name, then sighed and flopped on to a pile of sweatshirts. It had been a long day, and I was tired. I hoped I'd be going home to the boy soon.

A tiny knock at the door made Todd jump up as though one of his firecrackers had gone off right under him. I jumped up, too, and came over to stand right behind Todd as he whispered angrily out of his door at Linda.

I could smell the girl more than I could see her in the dark hallway. Her dress needed washing, and she had been eating salty crackers, and she was both worried and scared. That made me worried, too. I backed away from Todd and started to pace. I didn't feel like lying back down.

Todd slammed the door and locked it again. I could feel a flash of pure rage from him, and it frightened me. I'd felt the boy get angry from time to time, Dad and Mum, too. But that was a mild feeling compared to what I could sense from Todd.

Just then there was a drawn-out cry from outside the window. 'Bay-leecccc!'

Ethan! My boy was calling me!

I ran to the window and tried to jump up, putting both feet on the sill. But before I could see anything except that it was starting to get dark out there, Todd was beside me. He yanked a thick curtain that smelt of dust across the glass.

I couldn't see the boy! I barked in frustration. Todd smacked at my rear end with an open palm. 'No! Bad dog! No barking!'

I whined and backed away, as alarmed by the flare of rage and the tone of his voice as I was by the pain from my hindquarters. Had I been a bad dog? But I'd been trying to get to my boy! When he called, I was supposed to come!

'Todd?' a woman shouted from somewhere in the house.

Todd glared at me. 'You stay here. You *stay*,' he ordered. He backed out of the room, slamming the door behind him.

I paced around the room some more, confused. I knew the word 'Stay'. I knew what it meant. But I didn't like it much . . . and the boy was calling me! How could I find him? It wasn't right, being here in this room. I was becoming more and more sure about that. But the door was shut, and the window was covered, and Todd had certainly seemed angry when I'd barked . . .

A *click* came from the door, and I whirled around.

The door was eased open just a little, and in the narrow crack along its frame I could see Linda's face. She thrust a hand into the room. It was holding a soggy cracker.

'Here, Bailey,' she whispered. 'Good dog.'

I liked her voice, I liked her words, and most of all I liked that cracker. I was at the door in three steps, and I slurped the cracker out of her sweaty hand.

Linda opened the door wider and beckoned to me. I bounded down the hallway after her until we reached the kitchen. Todd's voice came from the living room. 'What? What do you *want*? No way. I'm not doing that.' A woman's voice mumbled. 'I don't care. I'm busy,' Todd snapped.

Linda and I had reached the door to the outside. She pushed it open and the cool night air flowed in. I sniffed it in gratefully and leaped on to the grass.

Then I turned to look back for a moment. Linda stood in the doorway, looking both relieved and miserable. For a moment I wished I could bring her with me. She seemed nice, and maybe she'd bring some crackers along with her.

Then I raced off into the night to find my boy.

Mum's car was down the street, and the boy was leaning out of a window, calling, 'Bay-leeeee!' I took off after it as fast as I could. The tail lights flashed brightly, and a moment later Ethan was out on the street, running to me. 'Oh, Bailey, where have you been?' he said, burying his face in my fur. 'You're a bad, bad dog!'

I knew that being a bad dog was wrong, but the love pouring off of the boy was so strong. I couldn't help feeling that, right now, being a bad dog was somehow good.

I was so glad to be back home that I didn't even check the gate to the backyard for a few days. When I did feel adventurous again and managed to slip out, I stayed away from Todd's end of the street. And if I ever saw or smelt him playing in the creek, I was careful to slink into shadows or dash behind some bushes before he could see me.

I was learning new words every day. Besides being a good dog, and sometimes a bad dog, I was told that I was a big dog over and over. It seemed to be a good thing, mostly, so I wagged when I heard it. I also noticed that I had trouble arranging myself comfortably on the boy's bed.

Then there was the word 'snow'. The first time I heard it, I thought Ethan was shouting 'No!' and I didn't understand. I didn't even have anything in my mouth! And I certainly hadn't lifted my leg. I'd already decided doing that inside the house was more trouble than it was worth.

But Ethan threw on his coat and hat and boots and dashed outside, yelling at me to follow. That's when I discovered that 'snow' meant the world outside had changed.

It was covered all over in a cold, white, furry coat. I paused at the back door and stared. Where had the grass gone? Where was the patio? I put a paw tentatively into the white fuzz. Cold! But Ethan was running around in it, and I wanted to be near him. So, very bravely, I jumped into the freezing stuff with all four feet.

'Come on, Bailey!' Ethan shouted. 'It's snow!'

The snow made my paws ache after a while, but it was fun to bite, and Ethan loved it so much that I decided I loved it, too. He pulled a heavy, flat wooden thing out of the garage. 'Let's go sledging, Bailey!' he said.

I followed him, tromping through the snow and up to a hill a few blocks from our house. He dropped the flat wooden thing to the ground and flopped down on top of it. 'It's a sledge, OK, Bailey? You watch, Bailey. It's fun!'

He pushed hard with his hands, and suddenly he shot down the hill, away from me.

I stared in astonishment. I never knew that the boy could move like that! Instead of walking or running stiffly upright on two legs, he was zooming close to the ground. I tore down the hill after him, barking with excitement and surprise.

The sledge slowed a bit as it got closer to the bottom of the hill, and that meant I could catch up. I timed things carefully and leaped, landing right on top of Ethan. He shouted. The sledge shot ahead, skimming past the sledges of several other children who had all been doing the same thing.

The ground flattened out and the sledge skidded sideways, tumbling Ethan and me off into a thick patch of snow. 'You like sledging!' Ethan gasped, laughing under me. 'You're a sledge dog, Bailey!'

I barked, and we raced up the hill to do it again.

We went sledging a lot while the snow stayed on the ground. After a while it went away, and I learned the word 'spring', which meant the sun stayed out longer, and the air warmed up, and Mum spent weekends digging in the backyard and planting flowers. The dirt smelt so wonderful, rich and dark and full of life, that after everybody went away, I dug, too, pulling the flowers back up from their beds. I hoped Mum appreciated my help.

That night they all called me a bad dog again, and I even had to spend the evening out in the garage instead of lying on Ethan's feet while he worked on his papers. I didn't understand it at all. I'd just done what Mum had been doing! What was wrong with that?

Then one day the kids on the school bus were so loud that I could hear them shrieking five minutes before the thing stopped in front of the house. The boy was full of joy as he ran up to me, so excited that I ran around and around in circles, barking as loud as I could.

When Mum came home, she was happy, too, and from then on Ethan didn't go to school any more. We got to lie in bed quietly every morning, instead of getting up for breakfast with Dad. Life had finally got back to normal. Thank goodness that whole school thing was over and done with.

8

One warm day, Ethan and Mum and Dad loaded up the car with a lot of suitcases and boxes, and then they called to me. I hopped into the back seat with Ethan. We took a long ride, and when we were done, we were at 'the farm'.

The farm meant new animals, new people and new smells. From the first moment I jumped out of the car after Ethan, I was very busy.

Two older people came out of a big white house, and there was a lot of happy exclaiming while I ran around everybody's feet. Ethan called the two new people Grandma and Grandpa. After he'd spent some time hugging them and hearing things like 'You've grown so *much*!' and 'So this is Bailey!' he ran off across a patch of packed-down dirt. 'Come on, Bailey!' he called to me.

He didn't need to call; I was already racing after him.

He took me past a split-rail fence where an enormous horse stared at me. I crawled under the fence to bark and invite her to play, but she only puffed air out through her nostrils and went back to biting off mouthfuls of grass. Her loss! I dived back under the fence and took off after Ethan, who was happily shouting my name.

I followed him down to a pond. I guessed that was what the farm had instead of a creek. There was a family of ducks to bark at, and they splashed into the water, paddling away as I ran up. Unfair! The minute I stopped barking, they came back towards the bank, the mother in the lead and half a dozen little fluff balls behind her in a line. So of course I had to bark again. Back they all went into the water. Ducks looked to me to be about as useless as Smokey the cat.

'You crazy dog, Bailey!' Happiness was pouring out of Ethan's voice. 'Come on!'

We went running back to the big white house.

Dad left after a few days, but Mum stayed with us on the farm that whole summer. Ethan slept on the porch, and I slept right there with him, and no one even pretended that the arrangement should be different.

Grandpa liked to sit in a chair and scratch my ears. Grandma always seemed to be cooking in the kitchen, and she needed me to sample what she made. I was glad to do my part. The love from both of them made me squirm with joy.

Outside, there was no yard, only a big open field with a fence. The horse, whose name was Flare, stayed inside the fence all day, eating grass. It was a strange thing, though; I never saw her throw up once. She did leave big brown piles all over the field, which smelt interesting but tasted dry and bland. I only ate a couple of them.

Sometimes Flare went into a big, shabby old building called the barn, and the first time I followed her in there I discovered that the farm had a cat. What a disappointment! She crouched back in the shadows and jumped up high or ran away whenever I came near. Well, that made her a better cat than Smokey, at least.

Beyond the barn were woods that were fun to explore, and it was always worth checking out the pond to see if the ducks needed to be barked at. The boy liked the pond, too. He would put me in an old rowing boat and push it out into the water. Then he would pull out a pole with a string attached, stick a worm on the string, and drop the worm over the side. Sometimes he'd pull out a small, wriggling fish for me to bark at. Then he'd let it go.

'It's too little, Bailey,' he'd say. 'But one of these days I'm going to catch a big one.'

One afternoon, after we'd been at the farm a few weeks, Ethan was at a table and Mum was stretched out on a couch with a book, and Grandma had gone upstairs to lie on her bed, which meant that the kitchen didn't smell as good as usual. I decided to explore a little more of the woods.

I hadn't got very far when I caught sight of the black cat from the barn, waddling slowly away from me. Of course, I took off after her. It was funny . . . when I'd seen the cat in the barn, I didn't remember a white stripe down her back. Now she definitely had one.

She didn't run away from me as quickly as she had before, either. As I got closer, I realized that this was no cat after all. It was a new kind of animal! Excited, I barked and bowed down low on my front legs to invite her to play.

She turned and gave me a solemn look, her fluffy tail high up in the air. I let my own tail wave back and forth. Great! Although everything about the farm was wonderful, the one thing that was lacking was another dog to wrestle with or chase around. I did miss Marshmallow from time to time.

I jumped forward to give my new playmate a nudge with my nose.

The next thing I knew, a plume of horrible stink puffed into my face, sticking to my eyes and lips, choking my nose. I sprang back. What had just happened? Half blind, helpless, I retreated, stumbling over sticks and roots, making my way back to the house.

'Skunk!' Grandpa announced when I scratched at the back door to be let in. 'Oh, you're not coming in, Bailey!'

Mum came to stand behind Grandpa on the other side of the door. 'Bailey, did you get into a skunk? Ugh, you sure did!'

Was that the name of the stinky cat creature in the woods? Skunk? Why was everyone just staring at me, not letting me in? I wanted to roll on the carpets and rub some of this awful smell off my fur.

That didn't happen, though. Instead, the boy came out, wrinkling his nose. He took me around to the side of the yard, where he wet me down with a hose. When I tried to lick his face, he pushed me away. 'Yuck, Bailey. Skunk!' he said. His voice was so stern that I understood: the skunk had been bad.

Then he held my collar while Grandpa showed up with a basket of tomatoes from the garden. Together,

Grandpa and the boy squished the soft, warm tomatoes all over me, rubbing the tart-smelling juice into my fur.

What a thing to do! I shook myself, sending water and juice and tomato pulp flying. 'Bailey!' the boy yelped, and Grandpa laughed and groaned at the same time. 'He needs a bath now,' the old man said.

A bath? What was that? I couldn't remember. Was it something to eat? That would help to make up for all this ridiculous treatment!

But it turned out that a bath *wasn't* something to eat. Mum brought out some soap that smelt a little bit (not very much, I thought) like roses. Ethan rubbed the suds into my fur until I smelt like a cross between Mum, a flower garden, and a tomato.

I had never been so embarrassed in my life. And things didn't get much better after that.

Even once I was dry, I had to stay out on the porch. And when Ethan came out there to sleep, he kicked me out of his bed!

'You stink, Bailey,' he said.

I lay on the floor and tried a whimper or two, but Ethan didn't give in and let me climb up. So I just tried to sleep despite all of the strange, bewildering smells floating around.

When morning finally came, I gulped down breakfast – Ethan brought my food bowl out to the porch for me – and raced outside.

A good roll in the grass helped to rub some of those dreadful odours of my fur. And when I checked out the pond, I got lucky. Something was lying on the bank – a dead fish! It was small, but the smell was good and strong. I rolled in it over and over, twisting my back to get the scent ground in properly. It didn't help as much as I thought it would, though. Under the marvellous dead fish smell, I could still sense tomato and perfume and that horrible tang of skunk.

I needed to figure all of this out, so I headed back for the woods. Sure enough, my nose led me quickly to that skunk. I sniffed at her, hoping that I'd pick up some information that would explain what had been going on.

And the very same thing happened! She lifted up her tail, and from her rear end, of all places, another powerful blast of stink hit me right in the face.

I yelped and backed away as quickly as I could. What was going on? Couldn't that skunk tell I just wanted to play? And if she didn't feel like playing, why didn't she just run away or hide or jump up on something tall, like Smokey or the barn cat always did?

Shaking my head, blinking, I stumbled back out of the woods. 'Oh, Bailey!' Ethan moaned when I found him by the fence. 'You're kidding me!'

I was put through the whole thing again – the water

from the hose, tomatoes from the garden, and Mum's horrible fake-flowery soap. Was this going to be my life now? Every day? Would I ever be let back into the house, where Grandma's cooking smelt so delicious? Would I ever sleep in the bed next to my boy again?

'You are so stupid, Bailey!' the boy scolded as he scrubbed me.

Grandma was watching this time. 'Don't call him stupid. It's such an ugly word,' she said. 'And he's hardly more than a puppy. He didn't know what he was doing. Tell him . . . tell him he's a doodle. That's what my mother always called me when I was a little girl and I did something wrong.'

The boy faced me sternly. 'Bailey, you are a doodle. You are a doodle, doodle dog.' And then he laughed and Grandma laughed, but I was so miserable I could barely move my tail.

Just to show that skunk, I was going to ignore her. That would serve her right, after everything she'd put me through.

9

Over the next few days, the smells faded from my fur. And about the time I finally smelt like myself again, my family stopped behaving so strangely. They let me in the house, and I took over my job of tasting kitchen scraps. The boy called me doodle from time to time, but I could tell he wasn't angry when he did.

'Want to go fishing, doodle dog?' he'd ask, and we'd shove out in the rowing boat and pull tiny fish out of the water for a few hours.

One day a chilly breeze swept in from a cloudy sky. Ethan pulled on a shirt with a hood that covered his head, and he called me to go down to the pond. We had been fishing for a while, and I was starting to

way out of the pond with the effort. I had to reach Ethan!

When I got to the trail of bubbles, I followed the scent. It was much harder to get myself down this time because I hadn't dived out of the boat, so I was slower to reach the boy. As I was headed towards the bottom of the pond, I glimpsed him beneath me, coming up. I switched directions. Our heads broke free of the water and out into the air at the same time.

'Bailey!' Ethan called in delight. He tossed his rod into the boat. 'You are such a good dog, Bailey!'

I swam beside him as he pulled the boat over to the sand. He was all right! The water hadn't taken my boy away from me! I was so relieved that I danced and licked Ethan's face as he bent to pull the boat out of the pond.

'You really tried to save me, boy.' I followed him on to the sand and shook myself again. Then I sat, panting, as Ethan left the boat on the sand and settled down beside me to stroke my face. His touch was as warming as the sun.

The next day, the boy brought Grandpa down to the dock. I raced ahead of them to be sure the duck family was out of the water. The boy was wearing another shirt with a hood, this one light grey, and he paused next to Grandpa on the dock. I sat down, too. All three of us looked into the green water.

'You watch. He'll dive underwater, I promise,' the boy said.

'I'll believe it when I see it,' Grandpa replied.

Grandpa grabbed my collar. 'Go!' he shouted to Ethan.

The boy took off running. I strained to follow, and Grandpa let me go. Ethan sailed off the end of the dock with a huge splash. I skidded to a stop and barked, looking back at Grandpa.

'Go get him, Bailey!' Grandpa said.

I looked down at the frothy water where the boy had gone in. Then I looked at Grandpa again. He was old and moved pretty slowly, but I couldn't believe he was so daft that he wasn't going to do anything about this! The boy needed help! Again! Why was Grandpa just standing there?

I barked some more.

'Go on!' Grandpa urged me.

Did I have to do everything in this family? With one more bark, I dived off the end of the dock, swimming down towards the bottom, where I could just see Ethan's light shirt. I gripped his collar in my jaws and headed for air.

'See! He saved me!' the boy called when our heads broke the surface.

'Good boy, Bailey!' Grandpa and Ethan shouted together.

I was so happy with the praise and so relieved that Ethan was OK that I decided to take off after the ducks. They'd thought it was safe to get back in the water. I'd show them! I got so close to snapping off a few tail feathers that they flapped their wings and quacked. That meant I'd won.

We spent the rest of the afternoon playing Rescue Me. After a few more times, I got less worried, since Ethan always came back up. Still, he was so happy every time I hauled him to the surface that I did it again and again.

I couldn't see any reason why we'd ever leave the farm, but when Dad arrived a few days later and Mum started walking from room to room, opening drawers and pulling things out, I had a feeling that we were going to be moving once again.

I stuck close to Ethan in case he had any ideas of leaving me behind. He laughed at me, and finally he yelled, 'Car ride!'

I dashed outside and jumped in the back seat, hanging my head out of the window. The horse, Flare, stared over the fence, probably jealous because I could fit inside the car and she couldn't. Grandma and Grandpa hugged Ethan and me before we drove away.

The car took us back to our first house. I missed the farm, but it was good to smell the familiar smells once more and to meet the other kids and dogs in the neighbourhood again. We played games and I chased balls and wrestled with my friend Marshmallow. It was wonderful.

What happened the next day was not so wonderful.

Everybody got up early, and I was led out to the garage. Again! I thought the people in my family had learned their lesson. Why was this starting all over?

I ran out of the dog door into the backyard and checked to see that Mum and Ethan were really leaving. They were! Ethan climbed into the big school bus and Mum drove away.

This would never do.

I barked for a while, and Marshmallow answered from down the street, but that didn't help as much as you'd think. Since I couldn't think of what else to do, I went back inside and sniffed at the doghouse. I wasn't about to spend the day in *there*.

I saw Smokey's feet underneath the door that led back to the house. I put my nose to the crack and breathed in his scent, letting out a frustrated sigh. He didn't smell sorry for me at all.

I was a big dog now, bigger than I'd been the last time I'd been locked in the garage. The doorknob wasn't as far above my head as it used to be. As I looked at it, I remembered how I'd got out of the yard where I had lived with my mother. I put my front paws on the door, took the knob in my mouth, and twisted it.

Nothing happened.

I didn't give up, though. The knob was slippery in my mouth and the metal tasted bitter, but I tugged and pulled, wrestling with it, and suddenly there was a click.

The door opened!

10

Smokey had been sitting against the other side of the door, probably laughing at my struggles with the knob. But when the door swung open, he definitely wasn't laughing any more! His pupils grew dark and he turned and fled. Of course, I followed, skittering around a corner and barking when he jumped up on to a counter.

It was much better in the house than in the garage. It was warmer, and it smelt nicer, and best of all, there was a long flat box lying on the counter. Last night's pizza dinner had been delivered in that box, and Ethan had let me have his crust. Delicious! I jumped up to pat the box with my front paw, and it tumbled easily to the floor.

I ate it. Well, all of it that I could, and I shredded the parts that were too tough to chew. Smokey watched, looking disgusted, but I knew he was just jealous. Then I ate the cat food in his bowl, licking it shiny, just as I did when I played Clean the Plates with Ethan.

Normally I wasn't allowed to get up on the couch, but I figured that the usual rules didn't apply now, since I was here in the house by myself. So I hopped up and settled in for a nice nap in the sun, on warm cushions that smelt of Ethan and Mum and Dad. Unfortunately, they smelt of Smokey, too; I couldn't do anything about that.

Sometime later, I realized that the sun had moved. What a nuisance. I stretched and wriggled into a new sunny spot.

Then I heard a faint creak. I knew that sound well. It meant that one of the kitchen cupboards was opening.

I jumped off the couch, shook myself, and hurried into the kitchen to see what was happening. Smokey was on the counter again, and he had carefully reached up with one paw and opened a cupboard. I didn't know he could do that!

Then he did something even more interesting. He jumped *right inside* the cupboard! For the first time, I thought that there might be some good in being as small as a cat.

Smokey shifted inside the cupboard and looked down at me, as if he were thinking. I nibbled an itch at the base of my tail and then glanced up at him.

Smokey had been tugging at a plastic bag with one paw. Now he smacked it once, then twice. On the third smack, the bag tipped over, wobbled for a moment on the edge of the cupboard, and fell. It hit the counter and bounced on to the floor.

I pounced on it and bit it. The plastic split open, and wonderful, delicious, salty, crunchy things sprayed all over the kitchen floor. I got busy cleaning them up. Smokey watched me and then batted down another bag. I ripped this one open. It was full of sweet, doughy rolls.

I decided right there and then that I had been wrong about Smokey. I almost felt bad that I'd eaten his break-fast earlier. It was his own fault for letting it sit there in the bowl, of course, but even so . . . If I'd known he was going to be so nice to me, I would have left his food alone.

At least I would have tried to.

I nosed at a few of the lower cupboards, but I couldn't get them open myself. How did Smokey do it? I did manage to get my front paws up on the counter and tug down a loaf of bread in another plastic bag. I ate the bread and left the plastic alone.

The kitchen bin didn't have a lid, so it was easy to

get in there. A few of the things inside were not to my taste. There was some bitter black grit that coated my tongue when I gave it a lick, plus some eggshells and more bits of plastic. None of those were worth my time. But there was plenty that I liked – pizza crusts, leftover scrambled egg, a scrap of bacon fat. I chewed up the plastic afterwards, just because.

I was outside waiting when the bus arrived. Chelsea and Todd both got off, but there was no sign of the boy. That meant he would be arriving later, with Mum. I went back into the house, wandered upstairs, and pulled a few shoes out of Mum's closet. I didn't chew on them too much, though. I was feeling full from all of my snacks, and kind of sleepy.

I carried the shoes down with me to the living room in case I wanted them later, and stood for a while, trying to decide if I wanted another nap on the couch (but the sun wasn't shining on it any more) or in a patch of sun on the carpet (but it wasn't as soft as the couch). With a sigh, I chose the carpet and lay down restlessly. I wasn't quite sure it had been the right choice.

When Mum's car door slammed, I was awake in an instant. I tore through the house, into the garage, out the dog door, and into the backyard, so that nobody would know about my wonderful day inside the house. Ethan ran straight to the backyard to play with me.

Mum walked up the drive, her shoes clicking.

'I missed you, Bailey! Did you have fun today?' the boy asked me, scratching under my chin.

'Ethan! Come and look at what Bailey did!'

At the sound of my name, said in such a stern voice, my ears fell.

Ethan and I went into the house, and I came up to Mum, wagging my tail as hard as I could so that she would be happy again. She was holding something in her hand – one of the shredded plastic bags I had left on the kitchen floor.

'The door to the garage was open. Look at this!' Mum said. 'The cinnamon rolls, the crisps, a loaf of bread, everything in the bin . . . Bailey, you are a bad, bad dog.'

I hung my head. I hadn't done anything wrong, surely, but I could tell that Mum was mad at me. Ethan was, too, especially after Mum told him to pick up all the bits of plastic off the floor.

'How in the world did he even get up on the counter? He must have jumped,' Mum said.

'You are a bad dog. A bad, bad dog, Bailey,' Ethan told me again.

Smokey strolled into the kitchen, blinking his wide, dark eyes and leaping easily up on to the counter. And no one said a word to him! Mum even gave him a fresh bowl of cat food. Then she pushed a mop around on the floor, and the boy carried a bag of rubbish out to the garage.

'Bailey, that was bad,' the boy whispered to me again. Why was everybody still so upset? I looked up at Smokey, who was daintily picking at his dinner, away up on the counter where I couldn't reach. He was a bad, bad cat, and nobody even seemed to know it.

'Bailey!' Mum shrieked from the living room.

I guessed she had found her shoes.

After that day, whenever I was left in the garage, I tried the doorknob again. But the door never opened a second time. I spent my days in the backyard, waiting for my boy. In the afternoons and on the days he didn't have to go to school, we got to be together.

On many days, we also got to spend time with the other neighbourhood kids. But I noticed that none of them ever went to knock on the door of Todd's house. Sometimes I saw him walking down the street, but nobody called out to him. Most days he didn't come up to the group of kids, either. He'd duck inside his house or head for the woods and the creek, alone.

Those times he did come over to the other kids, something strange would happen. The children grew quieter and more excited at the same time. There was a nervousness about them, and it made me nervous, too. Marshmallow seemed to feel the same way. She would stick close to Chelsea's side whenever Todd was nearby.

Ethan didn't go to Todd's house any more, but Todd still came to ours now and then, usually when Ethan and I were out in the yard together. One day he hurried up to the gate, calling Ethan's name. 'Come out! I got something,' he said.

Ethan went through the gate, and I went with him. Todd was carrying a bag, and he opened it up to let Ethan peek inside. 'Eggs? What's the big deal about a carton of eggs?' Ethan asked.

Todd grinned and nodded across the street, where a bunch of small girls were playing a hopping game, jumping over and around some chalked lines on the pavement.

'Let's get them,' Todd said, grinning.

Ethan looked over at the girls and back at Todd. 'What? You mean, like . . . throw the eggs?'

'Yeah! Of course!' Todd's grin grew wider, and I could tell that his heart was beating faster.

'That's . . .' Ethan hesitated. 'No way, Todd. Geez. Linda's over there!'

Linda's dark pigtails flew as she jumped. She looked much happier than the last time I'd seen her, inside her house.

'So what?' Todd's grin was fading. A sneer was taking his place. 'She's a little crybaby. Are you going to be a baby, too? What's the big deal?'

Ethan shook his head. 'I just don't want to. You're the one making a big deal.'

I didn't like the surge of rage that came off Todd, the way a whoosh of steam and smell would come out of a pot in the kitchen when Mum lifted the lid. He snatched the carton of eggs out of the bag and took a step away from Ethan. Suddenly he threw the carton hard at Ethan's feet.

Ethan jumped back, and I did, too, but I came forward again at once. Rich yellow yolks and slippery whites were oozing from the broken carton and sliding all over the driveway. Clearly, this was a job for me. I went to work.

'Crybaby,' I heard Todd mutter, but I was too busy licking to look up and watch him go.

Ethan rubbed my head for a minute and then went into our backyard. He came back with a hose and sprayed what was left of the broken eggs down the driveway and into the gutter. He picked up the remains of the carton and threw it in the garbage.

After that, Todd didn't come over to our house any more.

Not during the day, anyway. But once, after the snow and the cold weather came again, I was out in the backyard before bed, finding the right spot to use, when I smelt Todd on the other side of the fence. His smell was strong. He must have been there for quite a while. I let out a warning bark and was pretty pleased when I heard him turn around and run away.

11

I waited patiently for school to be over and done with. And finally it happened – the snow melted, the warm weather came, and one day Ethan jumped off the bus with extra excitement. A few days later, we were off to the farm.

The second that the car stopped, I leaped out, racing around the yard, quickly marking my territory in case any other dogs had got the wrong idea while I'd been gone. I greeted Flare and barked at the black cat in the barn and the ducks by the pond. They'd produced another batch of ducklings, although I could not imagine why. I raced into the woods, got a whiff of the skunk, and raced back out again. If she wanted to play, she knew where to find me.

I loved it at the farm, and I loved the happiness that poured out of Ethan when we were there. That second summer, there was one particular night Ethan was happier, more excited, and more anxious than usual. When it was bedtime, he didn't head for the sleeping porch as he usually did. Mum and Grandpa and Grandma didn't go upstairs, either. Instead, they all gathered in the living room. I stayed close. They might need my help.

Everybody stared at the television, although I couldn't see or smell anything interesting in the small, flickering images. Ethan's excitement spiralled up and up. Mum and Grandma and Grandpa were excited, too, and scared as well. Pretty soon I was going to have to bark, just to share in the feelings.

Then suddenly, all four of them yelled and cheered, and I barked, and nobody told me not to do it inside the house. Then Ethan took me out into the yard, and we sat down and looked up at the moon.

'There's a man up there right now, Bailey,' Ethan told me. 'See the moon? Some day I'll go there, too.'

He was so happy that I ran off and got a stick for him to throw for me. He laughed.

'Don't worry, Bailey. I'll take you with me when I go.'

Most days on the farm we did just what we had done the last year – fished in the pond or played Rescue Me, and wandered in the woods, and I did my tasting jobs in the kitchen. Sometimes Grandpa would drive into town, and he'd ask Ethan if he wanted to go. The boy would say yes, and I'd jump into the car with him.

Grandpa liked to go to a place where he sat in a chair and a man played with his hair. There were not enough other boys or dogs there, and Ethan would get bored. We'd end up walking up and down the streets, looking at windows and hoping to find some friends for me to sniff.

The best place to find other dogs was in the park. There was a big grassy area, and a pond, although we never played Rescue Me there. One day we spotted an older boy and his dog. The dog was a female, short, black, and all businesslike. When I trotted up to sniff her, she didn't even glance at me. Her eyes were on the thin plastic disc the boy was holding in his hand.

Then the boy threw it.

The dog raced and leaped and caught the disc before it even hit the ground. Pretty impressive, I suppose. If you like that sort of thing.

'What do you think, Bailey? Do you want to do that, boy?' Ethan asked, his eyes shining.

I found a stick to chew. I bet it tasted better than that plastic thing, anyway. When we got home, Ethan went right up to his room and got busy making something he called the flip.

'It's like a cross between a boomerang, a Frisbee, and a baseball,' he told Grandpa when he was finished. 'It will fly twice as far, because the ball gives it weight, see?'

I sniffed at the thing in his hand, which had been a perfectly good football before Ethan cut it up and asked Grandma to put some new stitches in it. 'Come on, Bailey!' Ethan shouted, running outside. Grandpa and I followed.

'How much money can you make on an invention like this?' Ethan asked eagerly.

'Let's just see how she flies,' Grandpa said.

'OK, ready, Bailey? Ready?'

I figured something was about to happen and stood alertly, my ears pricked to catch all sounds, my tail beating steadily. The boy cranked his arm back and flung the flip into the air, where it twisted and fell from the sky as if it had hit something.

I trotted over to sniff at it.

'Bring the flip, Bailey!' the boy called.

Gingerly, I picked the thing up. I remembered the short black dog chasing the plastic disc in the park and felt a little jealous. That disc had soared, and the dog had soared up to meet it. This thing – well, it didn't soar.

I took it back over to where the boy was standing and spat it out.

'Not aerodynamic,' Grandpa was saying. 'Too much resistance. It has to sort of slice through the air.'

'I just need to throw it right,' the boy insisted.

Grandpa went back inside, and for the next hour the boy threw the flip again. And again. And again.

I could sense frustration building in him, so after the tenth throw I left the flip where it had fallen and brought back a stick instead. I figured it would be more fun to throw, and it would definitely be more fun for me to catch.

'No, Bailey,' he said sadly. 'The flip. Get the flip!'

I barked, wagging, trying to get him to see how much fun the stick would be if he just gave it a chance.

'Bailey! The flip!'

And then someone said, 'Hi.' Ethan's head jerked around. The person who had spoken was a girl, about Ethan's age, I'd guess, standing next to a bicycle. I trotted over, wagging, and she patted my head.

In one hand she had a basket with something inside it that smelt sweet and dark and rich. I knew that smell; it was called chocolate. But I'd never been allowed to eat any. I sat down, trying hard to look as nice as possible, so she'd hand the basket over to me.

'What's your name, girl?' she asked me.

'He's a boy,' Ethan said. 'His name is Bailey.'

I looked over at the boy, because he'd said my name. I noticed something odd about him. It was almost as if he were afraid, but not exactly, even though he'd taken half a step backward when he saw the girl. I looked back at the girl. I liked her and her chocolate smell. I wagged.

'I live down the road. My mum made some brownies for your family,' the girl said, gesturing at her basket with her free hand.

'Oh,' the boy said.

I kept my attention on the basket.

'So, um . . .' the girl said.

'I'll get my grandmother,' the boy said. He turned and walked inside the house, but I decided to stay with the basket. And the girl, of course.

'Hi, Bailey, are you a good dog? You're a good dog,' the girl told me.

Good, but not good enough to get some chocolate, I discovered, even when I gave the basket a nudge with my nose so she'd get the hint. She just laughed and shook her head. Her hair was light-coloured and long enough to wave back and forth when she did that. She, too, seemed the tiniest bit afraid. Of what? The only thing around here that might make anyone anxious was a poor starving dog who needed a treat.

'Hannah!' Grandma said, coming out of the house. 'It's so good to see you.'

'Hi, Mrs Morgan.'

'Come in, come in. What have you got there?'

'My mum made some brownies.' I followed Hannah into the house.

'Well, isn't that wonderful,' Grandma went on. 'Ethan, you probably don't remember, but you and Hannah used to play together when you were just babies. She's a little more than a year younger than you.'

'I don't remember,' Ethan said, kicking at the carpet.

He was still acting oddly. He didn't seem to be in trouble, though, so I took on the duty of guarding Hannah's basket. Grandma set it on a side table next to Grandpa, who was in a chair with a book. He looked at the basket over the top of his glasses and reached in.

'Do not spoil your dinner!' Grandma hissed at him. He snatched his hand back. I looked at him with sympathy, and he looked back at me the same way. Nobody ever let us have any fun.

For the next several minutes, Grandma did most of the talking, Ethan stood with his hands in his pockets, and Hannah sat on the couch and didn't look at him. Nobody ate a treat. Finally, Ethan asked Hannah if she wanted to see the flip.

At the sound of that horrible word, I whipped my head around to stare at the boy in dismay. I thought we'd moved on. Could it be true that we weren't done throwing that horrible thing around?

The three of us went out into the yard. Ethan showed Hannah the flip, but when he threw it, it still fell to the ground like a dead bird.

'I need to make some design changes to it,' Ethan said.

I walked over to the flip but didn't pick it up, hoping the boy would decide to end the embarrassment once and for all.

Hannah stayed for a while. She went over to the pond to have a look at those stupid ducks, petted Flare on the nose, and took a couple of turns with the flip. Then she got on her bicycle, and as she steered down the driveway, I trotted beside her. The boy whistled for me and I returned at a dead run.

Something told me we'd be seeing that girl again. Maybe she'd bring the basket back with her, too.

12

Later that summer, the packing began again. Mum walked from room to room, but Ethan stayed on his bed, reading a book. I followed Mum for a bit as she put things in the car, and then came back to check on Ethan, confused. He put down his book and we both went outside.

Grandma and Grandpa had come out to the car, too. Ethan and I stood next to it as they both got inside.

'I'll navigate,' Grandpa said.

'You'll fall asleep before we cross the county line,' Grandma replied.

Mum wrapped the boy up in her arms. 'Now, Ethan. You are a big boy. You be good. You call if you have any problems.'

Ethan squirmed under his mother's hug. 'I know,' he said.

'We'll be back in two days. You need anything, you can ask Mr Huntley next door. I made you a casserole.'

'I know!' Ethan said.

'Bailey, you take good care of Ethan, hear?'

I wagged my tail. Were we going for a car ride or what?

'I stayed by myself all the time when I was his age,' Grandpa said. 'This will be good for him.'

I could feel worry and hesitation in Mum, but she let go of Ethan and got behind the wheel. 'I love you, Ethan,' she said.

Ethan mumbled something, kicking at the dirt.

The car rolled off down the driveway, and Ethan and I solemnly watched until it was out of sight. Then . . .

'Come on, Bailey!' Ethan shouted.

Everything was suddenly more fun. The boy ate some lunch, and when he was done we played Clean the Plate. We went into the barn, and he climbed up on the rafters while I barked, and when he jumped off into a pile of hay, I tackled him. An inky shadow from the corner told me the cat was watching all of this, but when I trotted over to see what she was doing, she slunk away and vanished.

When the afternoon grew late, the boy gave Flare

a bucketful of food, and we went back into the kitchen. He got some chicken out of the refrigerator and then, to my surprise, he took the plate into the living room. I followed him and watched with interest as he switched on the television and settled down in a chair, his plate on his lap. This was new! And it got even better when the boy tossed me bits of succulent chicken skin while he ate.

After we played Clean the Plate (twice in one day!), I decided to see just how much the rules had changed. I put a paw up on Grandpa's chair. The boy didn't say anything. I jumped up and looked over at the boy again. He glanced at me, smiled, and returned his eyes to the television.

After a bit, I heard the telephone ring, and I opened one eye to watch the boy get up to answer it. I heard him say, 'Bed,' but after he hung up the phone, he didn't go to the sleeping porch. He went back to his chair and the television, so I curled up a little tighter in mine.

I was in a solid sleep when a sudden sense of something wrong woke me with a jolt. I picked up my head. The boy was sitting stiffly upright, his head cocked.

'Did you hear a noise?' he whispered.

This seemed serious.

I got off the chair, stretched, shook, and looked at Ethan expectantly. What did he want me to do? When he didn't move, I went over to his chair. He touched my head, and his fear leaped from his skin. 'Bailey,' he whispered.

I wasn't at all sure what was happening, but I knew there was a threat somewhere. I prepared myself to face it, feeling the fur rising on my back and a growl forming in my throat.

Slowly, the boy stood up and took hold of my collar. I stayed close by him, on high alert, as we walked upstairs to Mum's room.

I could smell Mum strongly here, her sweat, the flowery soap she liked to use, her gentleness. Once the door was closed behind Ethan, I could feel him relax a little. So I did, too. He let go of my collar and looked around the room.

'OK,' he muttered.

He got on one side of the dresser and pushed with all his strength. It skidded across the floor. I watched, puzzled, as he pushed the heavy piece of furniture in front of the door. Hadn't he liked it where it was?

When the door was blocked, Ethan nodded, and I felt his fear die away. Whatever the threat had been, it seemed to have passed. Ethan pulled off his shoes and trousers and flopped down on the bed. 'Here, Bailey!' he called.

I jumped up and lay right beside him, and he hugged me tightly, both arms around me, the way he would do now and then in the doghouse. I licked his chin, which still tasted a little of chicken, and his ear. Then I settled down with my head across his chest, trying to be as comforting as I could.

We were together, after all. How could anything be wrong?

The next morning, we slept in and then had a fabulous breakfast. Ethan's fear from the night before was totally gone. I ate toast crusts and licked scrambled eggs and finished Ethan's milk for him. What a great day!

Ethan stayed in the kitchen after we played Clean the Plate, packing up more food and putting it into a bag, along with a bottle that he filled with water. He slid the whole thing into his backpack.

Were we going for a walk? A walk with food? I danced around the kitchen with excitement. Sometimes Ethan and I would go for long walks, and he'd bring sandwiches along for us to share. Lately, all of our walks seemed to take us down by the house where that girl, Hannah, lived. I could smell her scent on the mailbox. The boy would stand and look at her house, and then we'd turn around and walk home.

Whistling, the boy went out to take care of Flare, bringing her a bucket of dry seeds. I sniffed at them and licked a few, just to try them. They had no taste at all.

I was surprised when, after Flare had eaten, Ethan

fetched a blanket and a shiny leather saddle and put them on the horse's back. We'd done this a few times before, with Ethan climbing up to sit high on Flare's back while I watched from the ground. But it had always been with Grandpa there, and always with the gate to Flare's big yard firmly closed.

Today the boy opened the gate and then hoisted himself up on to the horse with a grin.

'Let's go, Bailey!' he called down to me.

I followed grumpily. I didn't like it that Flare was suddenly getting all of the boy's attention. I was so far away from Ethan, too, forced to walk beside this huge creature that I thought was about as dumb as the ducks.

Soon we were in the woods, walking along a trail. I spotted a rabbit and took off after it. I would have caught it, too, if it hadn't cheated by changing direction all of a sudden. I smelt more than one skunk, but of course I didn't go in their direction. Those skunks weren't worth my time.

We stopped at a small pool, and Ethan got off the horse. Both Flare and I took a drink, and Ethan ate sandwiches, tossing me the crusts.

'Isn't this great, Bailey? Are you having a good time?'

I watched his hand. Was he asking me if I was ready for more sandwiches? Of course I was.

It was nice to be out in the woods, even if Flare did have to tag along. Ethan hadn't brought the flip with him, so that was one good thing. And there were so many interesting smells, plus, of course, my boy. Ethan packed up the leftover sandwiches and got back up on Flare. We kept going.

We were so far from home by now that I could not smell any sign of it. I could tell that Ethan was getting tired from his voice and the way he sat on Flare. 'Do we go this way? Or that way?' he asked after we'd been riding for a while. 'Do you remember, Bailey? Do you know where we are?'

I looked up at him and wagged, and we kept walking. Ethan nudged Flare down a new trail.

I'd marked so much new territory that my leg was getting sore from being hoisted up into the air. And then Flare suddenly lifted her tail and let loose a huge gush of urine. What a stupid thing to do! Now her scent would wipe mine out, and nobody could smell me. Since I was the dog, that wasn't right! The horse should have known better. I wandered up ahead to clear the smell from my nose.

I topped a small rise, and that's when I saw the snake. It was coiled in a patch of sun, sticking its tongue out and in, out and in. I stopped, fascinated. I'd never seen one before.

'What is it, Bailey? What do you see?'

Whatever the boy was saying, it probably wasn't *Go bite the snake*. I didn't think it was the kind of thing I wanted to play with. Suppose it turned out to be like the skunk and had no idea how to play properly?

I ran back to the boy and Flare, keeping pace with them up the small hill. I wondered how Flare would react when she saw the snake curled up in front of her.

At first she *didn't* see it, but as she got closer, the snake suddenly pulled back, lifting its slim, dark head. And that's when Flare screamed.

I didn't even know that a horse could *make* that sound! It startled me so much that I jumped into a bush and barked wildly. Flare's front legs came off the ground, and she spun, kicking. The boy went flying off her back and hit the flat, packed dirt of the trail with a thump.

I ran to him at once. He sat up slowly, took a deep breath, and then jumped to his feet. He was OK! I danced happily around him, but he wasn't interested in playing. 'Flare!' he shouted.

The horse was already running at a full gallop down the trail the way we had come, her hooves pounding the dirt. The boy took off after her, and then I understood what needed to be done. I glanced back at the snake – it seemed to have disappeared – and then I chased Ethan, who was chasing Flare. Obviously this was a race, and Ethan and I had to win!

We didn't, though. I tore past Ethan, trying to keep up with Flare, but she was too fast and I was getting too far away from my boy. I turned back to be with him. He'd stopped running and was standing still.

'Oh no!' he was saying as I reached him, but I could tell that the 'no' wasn't for me. 'What are we going to do, Bailey?'

And the boy started crying.

13

These days, Ethan didn't cry as much as he had when he was younger. So I got worried, seeing his tears now. I shoved my face into his hands, trying to get as close as I could, trying to comfort him. That was my job.

The best thing, I decided, would be for us to go home and eat some more chicken.

The boy sat down on the path and cried some more, while I leaned on him and licked at his salty tears. At last he stopped and looked blankly around at the trees.

'We're lost, Bailey,' he said.

I wagged at the sound of my name. How about that chicken now?

The boy took off his backpack, reached in it for the

bottle of water, and took a gulp. Then he packed it away and got to his feet.

'Well, OK,' he said. 'Come on.'

Apparently our walk wasn't over, because he picked a new path and set out in a different direction.

We went a long way, and at one point we even crossed over our own scent, so I knew we had come in a circle. The boy kept plodding along, slow but determined. I grew slower, too. I was so tired that when a squirrel darted across the path in front of us, I didn't even bother to chase it.

When the light began to fade from the sky, we sat down on a log. Ethan ate the last of the sandwiches, and this time he didn't just give me the crusts; he let me have half a sandwich to myself, with tender turkey inside. Marvellous! I ate it in two gulps. Then he cupped his hand and dribbled water into it from the bottle for me to lap up.

'I'm really sorry, Bailey,' Ethan said.

Just before dark, the boy became interested in sticks. He began picking them up, carrying or dragging them to a tree that had fallen over. I hoped he might throw one or two, even though it would have been hard to dredge up the energy to chase them. But instead Ethan leaned all of the sticks against the wall of mud and gnarly roots that had been pulled up when the tree fell.

He piled pine needles on the ground underneath the sticks, and then found some branches with needles still attached to heap on top of the lean-to. I watched with interest.

When it became too dark to see, he crawled under the sticks. 'Here, Bailey! Come here!'

I crawled in beside him, on top of the pine needles. It reminded me of the doghouse. Why couldn't we go back home and curl up in Grandpa's chair? This seemed like a strange place to spend the evening.

The boy started to shiver. I eased myself as close to him as I could and put my head on top of him. This was the way I used to sleep with my brothers and sisters when we were cold.

'Good dog, Bailey,' he told me.

I wagged once, my tail thumping into the sticks that made a roof over us.

Soon Ethan stopped shivering, and his breathing got slower. I wasn't perfectly comfortable, but I didn't move. I knew that I needed to keep the boy as warm as possible.

We were up before the birds started to call. We both marked our territory – I was surprised, because I'd never seen the boy mark before! – and Ethan pulled the paper sack that had been full of sandwiches out of his backpack.

I stuck my nose inside it hopefully. It still smelt

deliciously of bread and turkey, but it was empty. I licked it anyway.

'We'll save it in case we need to make a fire,' Ethan told me. I figured he was probably saying *We need more sandwiches*, and I thumped my tail on the ground in agreement. We should go home. There would definitely be more sandwiches at home.

Our walk on this second day was not as much fun as the first day had been. Not even close.

The hunger in my belly grew to be a sharp pain, and after we'd walked for a while, the boy cried again, sniffling for about an hour. I could feel anxiety soaking through him, and I stayed close, sitting on his feet. Then he stopped crying and just sat still, staring at me with glassy eyes. I really didn't like that. It didn't feel right.

I was worried about my boy. We needed to go home – now.

I licked him in the face, getting him wet from his chin to his eyebrows. It seemed to wake him up a little, and he got to his feet.

'You're right, Bailey. We can't just sit here,' he agreed. 'Come on.'

We came to a small stream, and I raced ahead to stick my nose in and lap and drink. The boy hurried up behind me and flopped down on his belly to do the same thing. The water helped dull the pain in my stomach, and it seemed to give the boy new energy. When we started off again, we followed the stream.

The water twisted and turned through the trees. Ahead, sunlight glimmered between their trunks, and Ethan looked up with interest. He moved a little faster, and we pushed under the heavy branches of a pine and into the clear light.

The stream ran through a grassy meadow. 'That's better, huh, Bailey?' Ethan said. But as we stepped out into the sun, something nipped my nose, and Ethan slapped at his cheek. 'Mosquitoes!' he said.

Even so, we didn't turn back. Ethan pulled the collar of his shirt tight around his neck, and we kept going. After a little while, the stream splashed down a tiny waterfall and led us back under the trees once again.

I saw Ethan's shoulders slump.

That night the boy didn't pick up sticks. He just piled up a heap of dead leaves beside a big rock and curled up, half on the leaves, half under them. He clung tight to me. I didn't leave him, even though I could smell something dead nearby, something I might have been able to eat. The boy needed my warmth more than ever.

The cold black air settled down around us. I knew Ethan's strength was fading away. He was tired, and terribly hungry, and he couldn't go on much longer, not like this.

I had never been so afraid.

The next morning, it seemed to take a long time for the boy to get to his feet and start walking. When a branch slapped him in the face, he didn't put up a hand to protect himself. He just sat down in a puddle of mud.

I smelt blood. The branch had cut Ethan's cheek. I sniffed at it.

'Go away, Bailey!' he yelled.

I felt anger and fear and pain flaring inside him, but I didn't back off. I stayed close, and I knew I had done the right thing when he buried his face in my neck and cried some more.

'We're lost, Bailey. I'm so sorry,' the boy whispered.

I wagged at my name.

After some time, the boy got up again, pressing a hand on my back to give himself a boost. We followed the stream some more.

It led us into a bog, where the boy sank up to his calves with each step. Each foot made a sucking sound as he pulled it out. With four feet to take my weight, I didn't sink as deeply, but I still felt the cool slick of the mud between my toes.

Bugs swarmed about our faces. I snapped at the air as they aimed for my eyes and ears. Ethan covered his face with his hands.

He stopped moving. The air left his lungs in a long, deep sigh.

Worried, I picked my way close to him
on his leg

He was giving up. I could feel it.

I barked, a giant, deep, booming bark tha
from somewhere deep inside me. It was so loud that it
startled both of us. Even the bugs scattered for half a
second before swarming back.

Ethan moved his hands a little way from his face.
He blinked at me.

I barked again.

'OK,' he said with a groan. He reached down to get
his hands covered with mud, and slathered it over his
face and neck. 'OK, you're right, Bailey. OK.'

Slowly, he pulled his left foot out of the mud and
took a step, letting it sink again.

It took us half the day to cross that swamp. When
we picked up the stream on the other side of the bog,
it was deeper and wider, and the water moved faster.
Soon another trickle joined it, and another.

Ethan and I gulped big mouthfuls of water at every
pool. Once, Ethan didn't get up after he'd knelt to
drink.

I eyed him closely. I barked.

'No, it's OK, boy,' he said softly, as if he didn't have
the energy to raise his voice. 'Let's just rest, huh,
Bailey? Let's rest a little. Then we'll go on.'

He napped while I watched over him, keeping him

..m, my head on his chest. I was tempted to go to sleep, too, but I knew that wasn't the right thing to do.

Even as a puppy I'd been sure that there was an important job for me out in the world. Now I'd found it. I had to protect my boy. That mattered even more than comforting him when he was sad. I was supposed to watch over him, stay close by when he was in trouble. My purpose was to keep him safe.

After what seemed like a long time, I got worried enough to stick my nose in Ethan's ear. Wasn't he ever going to wake up? He snorted and his eyes fluttered open.

'You're a good dog, Bailey,' he whispered, and forced himself to his feet.

I was almost too tired to wag.

It was late afternoon when the stream joined a river. The boy stood and looked blankly at the dark water for a while, then aimed downstream, trampling down grasses, pushing through thick groves of young trees.

Night was just starting to fall when I picked up a scent that wasn't grass or mud or leaves or squirrels or deer or skunk. It was a smell I had not come across in days – the smell of other people.

Ethan was shuffling along, his feet scuffing through the dirt. I darted ahead of him, my nose to the ground.

'Come on, Bailey,' he mumbled. 'Where are you going?'

My nose found what I knew must be there – a dirt path worn into the ground, the smell of human feet thick on it. Following me, Ethan stumbled over the path. I think he didn't even notice it.

I barked.

Ethan turned his head to look at me, and his gaze sharpened. 'Hey!' he exclaimed.

I trotted on ahead. The path led us along the riverbank, and I kept my nose down. I could tell that the last person to walk on the path had gone this way, the way the river was flowing. The smell of human beings was becoming stronger. More people had been here, and not so long ago.

Ethan stopped, so I went back to him. He was standing, staring, his mouth open.

'Wow,' he said.

Ahead of us, the path led to a bridge across the river.

As I watched, a figure broke free of the gloom, crossing the bridge, looking out over the railing. I could sense Ethan's heart start to beat faster.

Suddenly, his excitement tipped over into fear. He eased himself backward until he stood against the trunk of a tree, under the shadow of its branches.

His mood reminded me of the way he had felt on our first night alone at home. It seemed there was a threat somewhere, even if I could not tell exactly where.

I shrank to his side. I pricked up my ears, alert for

whatever might be a danger to my boy.

'Bailey!' Ethan whispered. 'Be quiet!'

'Hey!' the man on the bridge shouted.

I felt the boy stiffen, getting ready to run away. I didn't think he could really run, though. Whatever the threat was, we'd have to face it.

'Hey!' the man shouted again. 'Are you Ethan?'

14

The man on the bridge gave us a car ride. Ethan got to sit in the front, and I had to be in the back, but I stuck my head over Ethan's seat to rest my chin on his shoulder.

'We've been searching the whole state of Michigan for you, son,' the man said, and Ethan looked down. I could sense sadness in him, and shame, and even a little fear under his relief. I licked his ear to help.

The man drove us to a big building, and as soon as we stopped, Dad opened the car door and he and Mum hugged Ethan. Grandma and Grandpa were there, and everyone was happy, even though there were no dog treats of any kind. And it was definitely time for dog treats, or more sandwiches, or even just a great big heaping bowl of ordinary dog food.

The boy sat down in a chair with wheels, and a man started to push him towards the building. I raced to his side.

'Wait,' Ethan said, holding up a hand. He bent over to hug me tight. 'I'll be back soon, Bailey,' he whispered into my neck. 'You're a good dog. A good dog. The best!'

Then he let go, and Grandpa held my collar as the man pushed Ethan inside the building. I pulled and twisted against the hand holding me back. I needed to go to my boy! We'd been together every night in the woods, and in the swamp, and in the car after the man had picked us up. We should stay together now!

Just before the man pushed the boy through the doors, Ethan turned and waved at me. 'He's OK now, Bailey,' Grandpa told me, and his voice was deeper and more hoarse than usual. 'He's going to be OK.'

I felt calm from Grandpa, and Ethan didn't seem to be scared any more, so I relaxed a little. It still would have been better to go with the boy, but when Grandpa tugged me gently towards his car, I went with him.

Grandpa let me be a front-seat dog. And then something even better happened. We stopped at a place where a young woman reached in through the window to hand Grandpa a delicious-smelling bag. Salt. Grease.

Meat! My tongue came out and I drooled a little on the seat.

Grandpa didn't mind. He fed me dinner right there in the car, unwrapping hot sandwiches one after the other and giving them to me. He ate one, too.

'Don't tell Grandma about this,' he said.

When we got home, I was so surprised to see Flare standing in her yard, just like always, that I barked at her. 'Enough, Bailey!' Grandpa said, pulling the car to a stop. He took me inside the house.

The boy didn't come home that night.

Now that my belly was full of those sandwiches, I was so tired I could have flopped down on the carpet and slept without moving. But I didn't do that. Where was Ethan? What if he needed me? I paced the hall on my sore paws, until Dad yelled, 'Lie down, Bailey!'

I paused. I knew what 'lie down' meant, but it felt wrong to rest without the boy.

Still, if Dad said . . .

I walked up and down the hall a few more times and then went out to the porch. I climbed wearily up on to Ethan's bed and slept there, with my head on his pillow, where his scent was strongest.

The next day, a car drove up the driveway and Ethan got out with Mum. I raced out of the door and danced around him. He rubbed my ears, but he was not as happy as I was.

I stayed close to my boy while Dad talked to him, and Mum talked to him, and Grandpa talked to him some more. Grandma only kissed him, and rubbed his hair, and kissed him again.

The boy kept his head down. I knew what a scolding was, and I knew one was happening now. But nobody even mentioned the name Flare! How could that be? It was because nobody else had been there to see Flare run away, I realized. Nobody knew Flare was a bad horse. They all thought it was the boy's fault that we had got lost.

I was angry enough to want to go outside and bite the horse, but I didn't, of course. The thing was huge. Instead, I put my head on Ethan's knee. At least the boy had me.

After all the talking was over, the girl, Hannah, came to visit. She and Ethan sat on the porch and didn't talk much, just sort of mumbled and looked away from each other.

'Were you scared?' Hannah asked.

'No,' the boy said.

'I would have been scared.'

'Well, I wasn't.'

'Did you get cold at night?'

'Yeah, pretty much.'

'Oh.'

'Yeah.'

I looked from the boy to the girl, keeping my ears cocked for words like 'Bailey', 'car ride', or 'treat'. But I heard nothing like that, so I lay down between them and sighed. Hannah reached over to rub behind my ears.

Not everyone rubs behind the ears in just the right way. Some people are too rough; some do it so lightly it tickles. And almost nobody does it for long enough. But Hannah was naturally talented at ear rubbing. She was so good at it that I rolled over so she could try a tummy rub, too.

I decided that I liked this girl. I wished she'd visit more often. Maybe she could bring more of those chocolate treats.

Life at the farm went back to normal once Ethan was home again. And then, long before I was ready, Mum packed and we took the car ride that meant school was coming. When we pulled in the driveway at home, several of the children in the neighbourhood came running. Chelsea was there, but Marshmallow wasn't with her, and when Ethan took me over to her yard a few days later, all of Marshmallow's smells were old and fading. Chelsea cried a little, and I put my head in her lap. She hugged me.

I wished Marshmallow would come out so that we could chase and wrestle, but she didn't.

That winter, about the time when Dad put a tree

in the living room for Merry Christmas, Chelsea got a new puppy. They named her Duchess.

Duchess liked to play. And play. And play. She liked it so much that there were times I got annoyed if her sharp little teeth sank into my ear or pulled too hard at my fur. Then I'd give her a quick growl to make her stop. She'd blink at me with an innocent, puzzled face, and back off for a few seconds before she seemed to decide that I couldn't have meant it. And she'd leap at me again.

It was very irritating. I like playtime as much as the next dog, but sometimes a dog just wants to lie still near his boy.

In the spring, the boy kept saying 'go-kart'. In fact, all the children in the neighbourhood kept saying it. And they spent a lot of time working with wood, sawing and hammering and totally ignoring their dogs.

Dad and Ethan went to the garage every evening, and the two of them were so busy out there that, finally, I actually went into Ethan's closet and dug out that horrible flip. I brought it to the garage and laid it at his feet. Surely *that* would make him look up from those stupid pieces of wood!

But it didn't. I could have howled with frustration.

'See my go-kart, Bailey?' was all he said to me. 'It's going to go fast.'

Finally, one sunny day, the boy put the tools away.

He opened up the garage door and rode the go-kart like a sledge down the driveway.

I trotted beside him, thinking that we'd certainly been through a lot of bother just to go from the garage door to the street. But when he got there, Ethan got out of the go-kart and carried it back up to the garage to play with it some more!

I just could not see the point of all this. At least with the flip there was something you could chew.

A week or so later, on a day when there was no school, all the kids in the neighbourhood got out their go-karts and brought them to the hill a few blocks away, where we went in the winter to go sledging. Duchess was too young to come with us, but I went along with my boy.

Todd was there, and he laughed and said something about the go-kart that Chelsea was pushing. I could tell by the way she turned her head away that her feelings were hurt.

When all the children lined up their go-karts at the top of the hill, Todd's was next to Ethan's. What happened next was very startling.

Someone yelled, 'Go!' and all the go-karts moved at once! I was so surprised that, for a moment or two, I forgot to chase them.

The karts were bumping and rolling down the slope, going faster and faster. Todd had braced his feet on the ground to give his go-kart a big shove as he started, and he was in front. Chelsea's kart was bumbling along near the back. Ethan's was gathering speed and getting closer to Todd's.

I headed out after them, running as fast as I could to catch up with my boy. Finally, I understood what all the hammering and sawing and sanding was for. It was just like sledging, but without snow. It meant that all of us could go fast together!

I galloped along, wind flapping my ears, my tongue hanging out. I passed one kart after another. Then I was racing right behind Ethan. The only kart in front of his was Todd's.

At the bottom of the hill, Billy, Ethan's friend who smelt of peanut butter, was standing with a flag on a stick. Ethan's cart (and Todd's, too) was headed straight for him.

Just like I did in the winter, when the boy was lying on his sledge, I leaped, landing right on the back of Ethan's go-kart. The go-kart was a little trickier than the sledge. Ethan was sitting up, not lying down, so I couldn't land on him. I flopped against his back and the kart lurched under us. 'Bailey!' Ethan yelled. But he was laughing.

My weight and the force of my jump pushed his kart ahead faster than ever. We whizzed past Todd and then past Billy, who waved his flag.

He must be having fun, too.

The ground levelled out, and our kart slowed and stopped. Ethan squirmed around to hug me. 'Good dog, Bailey!' he told me. I wagged. Were we going to do it again?

All the other go-karts rolled up behind us, followed by the rest of the children, yelling and laughing. Billy came over and held Ethan's hand up in the air. He dropped the stick with the flag on it, and I picked it up, shaking it, dancing around and daring anyone to try and take it from me.

'Not fair, not fair!' Todd shouted.

The crowd of children grew quiet. A hot fury poured off Todd. He pushed other children aside and stood facing Ethan.

'The dog jumped on the kart! That's why you won. That doesn't count,' Todd insisted.

'So what? Bailey was just playing,' Chelsea said. She tensed as Todd moved his furious gaze to her.

'I would have caught you anyway,' Ethan said.

'Everybody who says Todd's right, say "aye"!' Billy called.

'Aye!' shouted Todd. But he shouted it alone, and as he looked around, his anger doubled.

'Everybody who says Ethan won, say "nay",' Billy said.

'Nay!' the rest of the children all shouted. It was so

loud that I dropped my stick in surprise. Ethan grinned, not taking his eyes off Todd.

Todd took a step forward. His fist bunched up and he swung, hitting Ethan right in the centre of the chest. Ethan jumped back, ducking a little, and then he lunged forward and tackled Todd. The two of them fell to the ground.

'Fight!' Billy yelled.

Ethan and Todd rolled over the ground together. I knew about wrestling, but when dogs tussled, there was no anger, no desire to hurt. Here it was different.

I jumped forward, but Chelsea reached out to grab my collar. 'No, Bailey. Stay!' she told me.

I squirmed and twisted, trying to slip loose. I liked Chelsea, but she didn't get to tell me to stay when my boy needed me!

Ethan was soon sitting on top of Todd, his hands braced on the other boy's shoulders. 'You give in?' Ethan demanded.

Todd looked away. Waves of humiliation and hate wafted off of him. Finally, he nodded. Ethan got off him and both boys got up, slapping dirt from their trousers. Chelsea's hand slackened on my collar.

I felt the sudden surge of rage from Todd, and he lunged, slamming both his hands on Ethan's shoulders. Ethan staggered and almost fell.

I was there beside him, ready to defend him. Ethan

straightened up slowly. He put a hand on my neck.

Ethan looked at Todd. Then Billy stepped forward.

'No,' Billy said. 'You gave in, Todd. That's it.'

'No,' Chelsea said.

'No,' some of the other children said. 'No.'

Todd looked around. Then he turned away, his fists clenched at his sides. Without speaking, without looking at anyone, he picked up his go-kart and headed back up the hill.

Once Todd was gone, the rest of the children dragged their karts back up the hill and rode them down, again and again. I rode with Ethan each time.

That night, Ethan was excited at dinner, talking rapidly to Mum and Dad, who smiled as they listened. It took the boy a long time to fall asleep, and after he finally did, he was restless enough that, at last, I slid off the bed to lie on the floor. This meant I wasn't deeply asleep when I heard a huge crash from downstairs.

'What was that?' the boy asked, sitting bolt upright in bed. He threw the covers back as lights came on outside the bedroom door.

'Ethan, stay in your room,' Dad called from the hallway. His voice was tight; he was tense, angry and afraid. 'Bailey, come.'

Obediently, I trotted downstairs after Dad. He moved cautiously and turned on the lights in the living room. 'Who's there?' he asked loudly.

The curtains that hung on either side of the front window blew in the wind. 'Don't come down with bare feet!' Dad shouted.

'What is it?' Mum asked from the top of the stairs.

'Someone threw a rock through our window. Stay back, Bailey.'

As Dad went out into the hall for a pair of shoes, I sniffed at the shards of glass on the floor. In among them was a rock. When I put my nose to it, I instantly recognized the smell.

Todd.

15

A year or so later, in the spring, Smokey the cat got sick. He lay around moaning and didn't protest when I put my nose down in his face to find out what was wrong. I could smell sickness, but even more than that, I could smell exhaustion. He was worn-out, his small body soft and limp. I licked him between the ears.

Mum opened a can of delicious tuna, but Smokey just turned his face away from it. So I helped by finishing it up. Then Mum took Smokey for a car ride. When they came back, she was sad. Probably it was because cats are no fun in a car.

A week or so later, Smokey died.

After dinner, the family went into the backyard,

where Ethan had dug a big hole. I helped, of course. They wrapped Smokey's body in a blanket and covered it with dirt.

Ethan and Mum cried a little. I nuzzled both of them to remind them not to be sad. I was still there, after all, and obviously I was a much better pet than Smokey.

That summer we did not go to the farm at all. Ethan and some friends from the neighbourhood would get up every day and go to people's houses, where they'd cut grass with loud lawnmowers. I would go with the boy each day – that was good! But he'd always tie my leash to a tree while he worked, and that wasn't so fun. I simply couldn't figure out why the boy wanted to push a loud, smelly lawnmower over the ground instead of roaming through the woods or playing Rescue Me in the pond.

When school started again, there were more changes. Mum would get home before Ethan did and come to let me in. The boy would arrive late, just before dinner, smelling of dirt, sweat and grass. On some nights we'd all pile into the car and go to a big yard, where Ethan would play chase and fetch on a wide lawn with a lot of other boys. 'Hey, Bailey, want to come to the football game?' Ethan would ask.

One very odd thing about this game was that a lot of people would sit or stand around, and they'd all yell and scream for no reason at all. It was confusing, but the tide of excitement that swept up from all those people made me wag frantically and tug at my leash.

The first time I went to one of the games, I spotted Ethan, jumping up to grab a ball in mid-air. Another boy grabbed him, and they both rolled on the grass.

As quick as I could, I leaped forward, and my leash slipped out of Mum's hand. 'Bailey!' she shouted.

I dodged around a group of girls, jumped over a family sitting on the ground, and tore on to the big lawn to play with my boy.

The ball had rolled out of Ethan's hands when he'd hit the ground. I grabbed it. It tasted a lot like the flip – yuck! – and was big for my mouth, but when I got my teeth into it pretty good, it sank down to a better size.

'Bailey!' Ethan yelled, rolling to his feet. 'Bailey, no! Bad dog!'

But he couldn't really have meant that I was a bad dog, because he was laughing. I danced away with the ball in my mouth, and when some of the other boys tried to get it back, we had a fantastic game of This Ball Is Mine all up and down the big lawn. Finally, Ethan stopped laughing and called to me as if he really meant it. I raced up to him, panting, and dropped the ball at his feet, waiting for him to throw it again so that we could play some more.

'Doodle dog, Bailey!' he told me. Mum came running to the lawn to take my leash again. And then for some reason she pulled me back to the side before Ethan could throw the ball!

'Bailey, you're a bad dog!' she said, but I could tell that she didn't mean it, either. She was trying hard not to laugh. She did keep a firm grip on my leash all the rest of the game, which wasn't fair. Why did the boys get to play and not me?

Chelsea's puppy, Duchess, grew up and learned how to behave, and we became good friends. When it snowed, Ethan and I went sledging; when the snow melted, we went for walks and played fetch. A couple of times the boy pulled the flip out of the closet and stared at it. Each time, I tried to make myself very small and quiet so that he wouldn't think of making me fetch the thing. Then he'd put the flip away with a sigh, and I'd thump my tail on the floor, relieved.

The next summer was another one where Ethan wanted to push lawnmowers rather than go to the farm. Such a shame. And when the weather turned cool again, there was more football. I never got to play again, though. Sometimes I'd whine a little with frustration when I could smell Ethan in the midst of those running, wrestling boys, but I wasn't allowed to run and wrestle with him. Mum would stroke my head, and I could feel that she understood.

One wonderful new thing almost made up for the football. Ethan started to take his own car rides! Most times he would take me with him, and I'd get to be a front-seat dog. I'd stand with my nose out the window, drinking in the fascinating rush of scents as he drove down the road.

When summer came around again, Ethan took both me and Mum on a car ride to the farm. At last!

Flare pretended not to recognize me, and I couldn't tell for sure if the ducks and ducklings down by the pond were a different set or the same ones from last time. But nothing else had changed at all. I sniffed for the skunk in the woods, checked out what Grandma was cooking in the kitchen, and leaped into the pond, coming back to shake myself all over the family, who were sitting on the front porch.

Nearly every day Ethan would work with Grandpa and some other men, hammering and sawing boards. At first I thought he must be building another go-kart, but after a while I figured out that they were putting together a new barn, right next to the old one (which had a big hole in the roof).

Hammering and sawing were not very interesting, so every day I kept an eye out for anything else that might be going on. That meant I was the first one to spot the woman coming up the driveway. I ran down, ready to bark if I needed to. When I got close enough, I recognized her smell – it was the girl, Hannah! She was almost all grown up!

'Hi there, Bailey!' She rubbed behind my ears. She was still very good at that. 'Did you miss me? Good boy!'

Ethan was coming out of the old barn with a board in his hands. He stopped.

'Oh. Hi. Hannah?'

'Hi, Ethan.'

Grandpa and the other men were grinning at each other. Ethan looked over his shoulder at them, and his cheeks turned hot. Then he set down his board and came over to where Hannah and I were standing.

'So, hi,' he said again.

'Hi.'

They looked away from each other. Hannah stopped scratching. I gave her hand a little nudge with my nose to remind her that the job was not finished.

'Come on in the house,' Ethan said.

For the rest of that summer, whenever I went for a car ride with Ethan, I noticed that the front seat of the car smelt like Hannah. In fact, sometimes

Ethan smelt like Hannah. That was probably because they liked to sit very close together when they could. One time I took a little nap on the rug while they were sitting right next to each other on the couch. Suddenly the excitement and alarm pouring out of both of them jerked me awake.

I jumped up, looking around to see what the matter was. Nothing seemed to be wrong. Ethan and Hannah didn't even look at me. Their faces were very close together, and their hearts were beating fast.

Quickly, I jumped up on to the couch, working my face between theirs, swiping Ethan's chin with my tongue, getting a bit of Hannah's cheek wet as well. I knew I wasn't supposed to be on the couch, but since something exciting was obviously happening, I figured the rules could be bent a bit. I'd need to be close at hand for whatever was going on.

Ethan and Hannah both burst out laughing, and all the excitement faded. I guessed nothing was going to happen after all. But they did let me stay on the couch with them while they watched a movie.

Then the day came when Mum began to walk around the house and carry things out to the car. That time, nobody was laughing.

There was a smell of new paint in the air from the barn. The girl came over, and she and Ethan walked down to the pond and sat on the dock, dangling their feet over the water. And they talked. And talked. And talked.

They didn't throw sticks or swim or do anything fun. I barked a bit at the ducks – I had the feeling it might be my last chance for a while – and came back to the pair of them to see if anything more interesting was going on.

There wasn't. Hannah was crying a little, and Ethan was hugging her. I gave her hand a nudge, but she didn't seem to be in the mood to rub ears, so I lay down and sighed. No ear rubs? No sticks? No treats? No games of Rescue Me?

There was more hugging at the car, and then we drove away, Ethan honking as we went.

16

Things were a little different at home once school began. For one thing, Ethan spent a lot of time in his room, talking on the phone. He kept saying 'Hannah', but I never did see or smell the girl, which was a shame. My ears could have used a really good rub.

The leaves were falling from the trees on the day that Ethan took me for a car ride to a place where big silver school buses came and went, and there was a stench of smoke and burned petrol in the air. Standing beside one of those buses, waving when she saw us, was Hannah!

I don't know who was more excited to see her, me or the boy. I wanted to play with her, but all the boy wanted to do was hug her. I wound my leash around their legs in excitement, and they had to stop hugging to get untangled, saying my name and laughing and stopping halfway through to hug again.

I was so glad to see Hannah that I didn't even mind being a backseat dog on the way home, while she got to sit next to Ethan. 'Coach says there will be football scouts from some colleges there to see me play tonight, Hannah,' the boy said. 'University of Michigan. Michigan State, too.' I could hear the excitement in his voice, and also a little fear. I looked out of the window to see what might be going on, but there was nothing unusual out there.

That night, I was proud to stay with Hannah while Ethan played football with his friends. I led her over to where Mum usually took me and showed her where to sit.

We'd only been there a little while when Todd came walking by.

'Hi, Bailey,' he said to me, his voice friendly. But something was still wrong about him. I sniffed the hand he held out but pulled my head away when he tried to pet me.

'Do you know Bailey?' the girl asked. I thumped my tail on her leg when I heard my name.

'We're old pals, aren't we, boy? Good dog.'

I did not need to be called a good dog by someone like Todd.

'You don't go to school here. Do you go to East High?' Todd asked.

'No, I'm just visiting Ethan's family.'

'What are you, a cousin or something?'

The people in the crowd all shouted, and I jerked my head around. More wrestling was happening out on the big lawn. I gave a little tug at the leash, but Mum must have told Hannah to keep a good hold of it. I wasn't going to get to play today, either.

'No,' Hannah told Todd. 'Just . . . a friend.'

'So you want to hang out?' Todd asked. 'Some of us are getting together. This game's going nowhere.'

'No, I . . . I'd better wait for Ethan.' I cocked my head towards the girl. I could sense her getting anxious, and I didn't blame her. Maybe she could feel the anger inside Todd, just the way I could. It was always there, and now it was starting to build.

I remembered the way his hand had come down on my hindquarters. I moved a little closer to the girl.

'Ethan!' Todd turned and spat in the grass. 'What, is he your boyfriend?'

'Well . . .'

''Cause you should know, he's pretty much going out with Michele Underwood. She's one of the cheerleaders.' Todd pointed. 'See, over there? With all the blond hair?'

'What?'

'Yeah. Like, everybody knows it.'

'Oh.'

Todd moved closer to the girl, and when she stiffened, I saw that his hand was touching her shoulder. Nervousness spiked inside her, and it brought me to my feet.

Todd looked down at me, and I felt the fur lifting on the back of my neck. Before I even knew I was going to do it, a low growl rose in my throat.

'Bailey!' The girl leaped up. 'What's the matter?'

Todd was looking at Hannah now, ignoring me. 'Why don't you tie up the dog and come with me? It'll be fun.'

'Um, no.' Hannah tugged at the zip on her jacket. 'No. I couldn't do that.'

'Why not? Come on.'

'No, I have to take care of Bailey.'

Todd shrugged. He stared at her. 'Yeah. Well, whatever.'

The anger inside him was a tide about to overflow. I growled again. This time the girl didn't say anything to me about it. She didn't say anything to Todd, either.

'Fine,' Todd said. 'You ask Ethan about Michele. OK? You ask him.' He jammed his hands into his pockets and walked away.

Hannah sat down and put an arm around me. I leaned against her. When the rest of the people around us shouted and yelled, she stayed quiet.

An hour or so later, Ethan ran up to us, sweaty and happy and excited. 'Michigan State, here we come!' he shouted. I wagged and barked and danced at the end of my leash. Then Ethan's happiness drained away as he looked at the girl.

'What's the matter, Hannah?'

'Who is Michele?'

I put my paw on Ethan's leg to let him know that I was ready to play with the football now, if he wanted. The other boys had left the big lawn, but I was right here.

'Michele? Who do you mean?' Ethan laughed, but the laughter stopped after a second, as if he had run out of air. 'Hannah? What's wrong?'

The boy and the girl walked in circles around the big yard, talking, talking, talking, while the other people left and the light faded and the air grew chillier. I trailed behind them, finding some worthwhile scraps on the ground – popcorn, crusts from a tuna sandwich, an ice-cream wrapper. I wondered why people thought that making sounds with their mouths was more fun than chasing a football or running around on a field.

'I don't know this girl,' Ethan said. 'Who said that to you?'

'I don't know his name. He knew Bailey, though.'

I froze at my name, and lifted my nose from the candy wrapper I was licking. But nobody seemed about to take it away from me. I went back to work.

'Everybody knows Bailey. He comes to all the games.'

More walking. More talking. But I'd already found most of the scraps worth eating, and I was ready to go home. Finally, the boy and the girl stopped and hugged each other. They certainly did that a lot.

'Want to go for a car ride, Bailey?' the boy asked.

Of course I did!

We went home, and there was *more* talking (didn't they ever get tired of that?) and some more hugging on the couch. I went into the backyard, leaving them to it, and found something remarkable there.

Meat. A big piece of meat lying right in the grass.

I was about to gulp it down before any other dog could come along and steal it, but I hesitated. I put my nose down for a second sniff.

It didn't smell quite right. There was a funny, bitter odour that I had never smelt on food before. Even more strange, Todd's scent was all over it.

I picked up the piece of meat and carried it over to the patio near the back door. Then I dropped it. It didn't just smell bitter; it tasted bitter, too. Foamy saliva rushed into my mouth and I let it dribble out on to the grass.

I sat down and looked at the meat.

It didn't smell right. It didn't taste right. But it *was* meat. Right here in my own yard. Maybe if I gulped it down fast, the bitter taste wouldn't be so bad.

I poked the meat with my nose and then lay down next to it, staring at it. Why did it smell so strongly of Todd?

17

When Mum came outside the next morning and saw me, I hung my head and flattened my ears. I felt guilty for some reason. But I wasn't sure why.

'Good morning, Bailey,' she said. Then she saw the meat. 'What's this?'

She bent over to look at the meat more closely. I tried a timid wag. The tip of my tail just brushed against the patio bricks. That meat had been worrying me all night. Should I have eaten it? Was it the right thing to leave it alone? What should I do to be a good dog?

When I rolled over and Mum rubbed my belly, I felt better. Bad dogs didn't get tummy rubs. 'Where did this come from, Bailey?' Mum stopped scratching and picked the piece of meat up gingerly between two fingers. 'Ugh,' she said.

I sat up and cocked my head. Was Mum going to feed me the meat? If she did that, it must be OK after all. My tail wagged more strongly.

'Yuck, Bailey. You don't want that, whatever it is,' Mum said. She dropped the meat into the bin.

Hannah sat in my front seat for the car ride to the giant silver school bus, and I was alone in the car for a long time while Ethan and Hannah stood and hugged. When the bus drove away and the boy came back to the car, I could sense his loneliness and wondered if he needed to go home and play Doghouse. I hopped into the front seat and lay down with my head in his lap instead of sticking my nose out of the window.

The girl came to visit again the day after the family sat around the indoor tree and tore up papers for Merry Christmas. Normally, I liked this time of year because I'd have Mum and Dad and Ethan together, in one room, with good smells coming from the kitchen and some paper for me to rip with my teeth. (The family didn't usually like it when I ripped up paper, but on Merry Christmas the rules were different.)

This year Christmas was not as much fun as usual, because Ethan gave Mum a new black-and-white kitten, named Felix. That little scrap of fur had no manners at all! He would stalk my tail from behind or leap out at me from behind the couch, batting at me with his tiny paws. When I tried to play with him, he wrapped his legs around my nose and nibbled me with his sharp teeth. He was worse than Duchess when she'd been a puppy! Finally, I shrank into a corner and put my nose down on my front paws with a long sigh to remind Ethan of how much I was suffering.

Even Hannah, when she arrived, paid far too much attention to Felix. I'd known her longer and, of course, I was her favourite pet. But she kept dangling bits of Christmas ribbon in front of the kitten's nose and laughing. I'd have to come up and nudge her hard with my nose to make her give me one of those good ear rubs.

At least I got to go outside with Hannah and Ethan. Felix tried once. He put one paw into the fluffy white snow that surrounded the house and then turned around and dashed straight inside as if he'd been burned. So when the boy and the girl built a big pile of snow in the front yard and put a hat on it, I was right there beside them. The boy liked to tackle me and drag me around in the white stuff, and I liked to let him, just for the joy of having his arms around me. It was how we'd played every day when we were both younger.

Her second day with us, Hannah and Ethan and I went sledging. Felix, of course, had to stay behind.

The sun was out, and the air was so cold and clean I could taste it all the way down my throat. Most of the children from the neighbourhood were there at the sledging hill, and Hannah and Ethan spent as much time pulling the younger ones up to the top as riding down themselves. I was at the bottom when Todd drove up.

He looked at me when he got out of the car, but he didn't hold out his hand or say anything to me. I kept my distance.

'Linda! Come on, time to come home!' he shouted.

Linda was on the slope with three of her little friends, sliding down on a round piece of plastic, spinning and giggling. Ethan and Hannah flashed past them, both lying on one sledge.

'No! I don't want to!' Linda yelled.

'Now! Mum says!'

Ethan and Hannah flopped off their sledge at the bottom of the hill, tumbling in the snow. I raced over and sniffed them, in case they smelt different now that they'd had a ride without me. Todd stood and watched them.

Something in Todd rose up to the surface, something worse than anger, something I'd never felt from anyone before. It was dark, scalding hot, and frightening. My head came up, and I felt a growl swelling in my throat.

Ethan and the girl stood up, wiping snow off of each other. Happiness was spilling off them. I looked back and forth from them to the other boy standing so still, his face a blank, his hands in his pockets, his shoulders hunched.

'Hey, Todd,' Ethan said, beaming.

'Hi.'

'This is Hannah. Hannah, this is Todd. He lives down the street.'

Hannah reached her hand out, smiling. 'Nice to meet you.'

Todd stiffened a little. 'Actually, we already met.'

Hannah pushed her purple knitted cap back a little from her eyes. 'We did?'

'At the football game,' Todd said. Then he laughed, a short bark. It sounded to me like a warning.

Hannah blinked. 'Oh. Oh, right,' she said.

'What?' Ethan asked.

'I have to pick up my sister,' Todd told them. 'Linda!' he yelled, cupping his hands to his mouth. 'Come home *now*!'

Linda's sledge had spun to a stop. She tugged herself out of a pile of friends and trudged through the snow towards Todd, her face downcast.

'He's . . . he's the one I talked to,' Hannah told

Ethan. Some worry flickered through her, and I felt it. I also felt the quick flare of anger from Ethan.

'Wait, what? You? Todd, you were the one who told Hannah I'm going out with Michele? I don't even *know* Michele.'

'I've got to go,' Todd mumbled. 'Get in the car, Linda.'

'No, wait,' Ethan said. He reached his hand out. Todd jerked away from it.

'Ethan,' Hannah murmured. She put a mittened hand on his arm.

'Why would you do that, Todd? Why would you lie? What's wrong with you, man?'

The emotions boiling inside Todd seemed hot enough to melt the snow he stood on, but his face didn't change. He stood there, not saying a word. I wanted to grip the hem of Ethan's jacket in my teeth and tug him away, but I knew that good dogs shouldn't do that.

'This is why you don't have any friends, Todd.' Hannah drew in a quick little breath when she heard Ethan's words. 'Why can't you just be normal? You're always doing stupid things like this. It's sick.'

Todd still said nothing. He simply walked away and got in his car. Linda was already in the back seat. He slammed the door.

Todd's face, looking out the window at Ethan and Hannah, was absolutely blank. Even the motor of the car sounded angry as he drove away.

'That was mean,' Hannah said.

'Oh, you don't know him.'

'I don't care. You shouldn't have said that he doesn't have any friends.'

'Well, he doesn't. He's always doing this kind of stuff. He's always been *twisted*, you know? Ever since we were kids. The kind of stuff he thinks is fun . . .' Ethan shook his head. 'Anyway, I don't care about Todd. Come on, we've got to get home.'

A few days after Hannah left, the snow came down and the wind blew so hard that we stayed inside all day, sitting in front of the heaters. That night, I slept *under* the covers on Ethan's bed. The next morning the snow finally stopped, and Ethan and I went out and dug for hours in the driveway, him with a shovel and me with my paws.

The moon came out right after dinner, so bright that I could see nearly as well as in the daytime. When I went out in the backyard, the air was thick and sweet with the smell of smoke from many different fire-places.

Ethan shut the door and went inside. Faintly I heard him call to Mum, 'I'm worn out from all that shovelling. I'm going to bed. Let Bailey in, OK?'

I didn't hear Mum answer him, because I had discovered something interesting about the fence.

The snow had drifted up against it, blown by the wind to make a smooth hill. It was easy to climb to the top of the hill, and from there it was only a short hop to the ground on the other side.

Time for a night-time adventure!

18

I went to Chelsea's house first, to see if Duchess was out, but there was no sign of her except a yellow patch on the snow near her front door. I lifted my own leg over the same place so that she'd know I was thinking of her.

Normally when I got outside the gate, I went for a stroll along the creek – except, of course, if I saw Todd there. But because of all the snow, tonight I had to stick to the ploughed road. Some people had already dragged their indoor trees outside, although at our house the tree still stood in the front window, glistening with lights and hung with shiny ornaments for Felix to attack. When I came across one of those discarded trees, I marked it with my scent. I could always smell just one more tree a little further down the road, and so I stayed out later than I'd ever done before.

If I hadn't gone so far, if I'd turned back just a little sooner, I might have been in time to stop what happened next.

Finally, a car turning into the street from a driveway up ahead blazed its headlights into my eyes. When it drove slowly by, the smell of it reminded me of the smell of Mum's car, those times she and Ethan would come looking for me. I felt guilty for being so far from my boy, so I lowered my head and trotted for home.

When I turned up the driveway where Ethan and I had dug that morning, I stopped. My eyes and my nose together noticed several things at once, all of them wrong.

The front door was open, and wafting out was the warm scent of home. But another scent was laid on top of that – something chemical, sharp, both unpleasant and familiar. I'd smelt it in the garage before, and on the car rides I took with the boy. Petrol.

That smell was so strong that it covered the scent of the person backing out of the open front door. All I had to rely on was my eyes, and in the moonlight, I thought I was looking at my boy. I trotted closer, just as the figure turned, tossing more petrol from a jug in his hand on to the bushes near the front door.

I stopped. Now I was close enough to catch the scent. Todd.

He hadn't seen me yet. The fur along my spine and neck rose as he took three steps back and pulled some paper from his pocket. From another pocket came a box of matches. There was a tiny scraping sound, and a flare of light popped up in Todd's hand, brightness flickering against his stony face.

He tossed the burning paper on to the bushes, and a blue flame swept up, making a soft whoosh in the quiet night-time air.

Todd didn't turn. He stood watching the fire. And I never barked, I never growled. I just raced up that pavement in silent fury.

I knew good dogs didn't jump on people. Good dogs didn't knock them down. Good dogs didn't bite.

But all of that didn't matter. Somehow, I knew that what Todd was doing was wrong. He was trying to hurt the boy and my family. I could tell it from the crackling heat of the fire, from its charred smell of danger, from the dark delight rising inside Todd as he stood watching the burning house.

Even more than staying close to the boy, playing with the boy, comforting the boy, my job was to keep the boy safe. I had done that in the woods. I would do it here.

I leaped for Todd as if I had a pack at my heels,

crashing into him with all of my weight, knocking him to the snow.

Todd yelled and thrashed underneath me, twisting and rolling. He kicked at my face. I snatched his foot in my mouth and held it, biting hard, holding on while Todd screamed. His trousers ripped, and his shoe came off in my mouth. I dropped the shoe, lunging forward to get a second grip on his foot with my teeth.

Yelling again, Todd hit at me with his fists, but I kept my jaws locked around his ankle, shaking my head as if he were prey. I'd never bitten anyone, not like this, but I didn't let go.

Then a shrill, piercing noise stabbed through the air. I jerked my head around to locate this new threat. Inside the house, I could see that the indoor tree was burning like a candle. Thick smoke poured out of the open front door.

Todd yanked his foot free, and I backed away, shaking my head. The noise hurt my ears and I wanted to run from it – but what about my boy?

Staggering to his feet, Todd limped away as fast as he could. I let him go, suddenly more worried than angry. I added my own alarm to the noise, barking and running from the front door to the driveway and back again. I pivoted and raced towards the back of the house, but the pile of snow that had helped me leap over the fence was on the wrong side. I couldn't get over, so all I could do was bark louder than ever.

While I stood there, making as much noise as I could, the back door opened. Black smoke poured out, and Mum and Dad came with it, coughing and hanging on to each other.

Mum spun back to face the open door. 'Ethan!' she screamed.

Dad pulled Mum towards the gate, and I met them there. They pushed the gate open against the snow and shoved past me, stumbling to the front of the house. They stood looking up at the dark windows of Ethan's room.

'Ethan!' they shouted. 'Ethan!'

I raced through the gate to the open back door. Felix the cat was on the patio, huddled under a bench. He yowled at me, but I didn't stop. I ran inside.

The heat wrapped itself around me and choked me. Smoke forced its way into my eyes and nose. Unable to see, unable to smell, I tried to stagger towards the stairs, but it was hard to tell which way to go.

The sound of the flames all around was as loud as the wind when we travelled in the car with the windows down. My nose bumped hard into something. A chair? A wall? I couldn't tell. I couldn't find the stairs! I couldn't find my boy!

Desperate for clean air, I sensed the coolness of the

open door behind me and ran for it. Outside again, the fresh night eased my stinging eyes and my burning nose.

Mum and Dad were still yelling. Lights had come on across the street and in the house next door. Through the window, I could see one of our neighbours talking on his phone.

'Ethan!' Mum and Dad shouted. 'Ethan!'

Fear was pouring off of Mum and Dad. Never, not even when Ethan and I were lost in the woods, have I felt an emotion so strong. Mum was sobbing, and Dad's voice was getting louder and tighter, and when I started to add my own frantic barking to the noise, no one told me to stop.

My ears picked up the thin wail of a siren, but it seemed to be far away. All of the other noise was faint beside the roar of the fire, a sound so deep and loud that I felt it as a vibration in my entire body. The snow in the yard was starting to melt, clouds of steam rising as the yard sizzled.

'Ethan! Please!' Dad shouted, his voice breaking into a sob.

Just then, something burst through Ethan's window, showering the yard with shards of glass. It landed with a plop in a mound of wet snow. The flip!

I raced to it and picked it up. That's what I was supposed to do, right? I'd show Ethan that I had the flip. He'd be happy.

Ethan's head appeared in the hole that the flip had made in the window. Black smoke puffed out around him.

'Mum!' he yelled. Coughs almost swallowed the words.

'You've got to get out of there, Ethan!' Dad roared.

'I can't open the window. It's stuck!'

'Just jump!' Dad answered.

'You've got to jump, honey!' Mum shouted.

The boy's head disappeared back inside. 'The smoke is going to kill him. What's he doing?' Dad asked, standing rigid, staring at Ethan's window. I ran to his side. With the flip in my mouth, I couldn't bark any more, but I wanted to. I wanted to make all the noise I could, race around the yard, do something with the terrible, frustrated energy building up inside me. But I didn't. I leaned on Dad's leg, trembling, waiting for my next sight of the boy.

'Ethan!' Mum screamed.

The boy's desk chair crashed through what was left of the window. A minute later, the boy followed. But something – a foot, a knee, maybe? – caught on the broken bits of wood and glass still in the window frame. And instead of sailing over the smouldering bushes and into the yard, Ethan flopped right into them.

I dropped the flip to bark madly. Mum and Dad

scrambled forward to drag Ethan on to the soggy grass, rolling him over until he lay on his back, his eyes closed.

'Are you OK, son? Are you OK?' Dad asked.

'My leg,' Ethan gasped, coughing.

I snatched up the flip and jumped to his side. My boy smelt burnt and bloody and hurt and frightened.

'Go away, Bailey,' Dad ordered.

The boy opened his eyes and grinned at me, reaching out a shaking hand. 'No, it's OK. Good dog, Bailey. You caught the flip. Good dog.'

19

I wanted to throw myself on Ethan, but I could tell that I shouldn't touch him. Instead, I put the flip down gently beside him. Then I lay down on the wet grass and inched forward so that my nose brushed his face.

Cars and trucks began arriving, lights flashing. Men ran up to the house and began spraying it with big hoses. More people brought over a bed on wheels and lifted the boy gently on to it. They rolled the bed over to a truck.

I trotted right at the side of the bed, and when the men opened two doors at the back of the truck and boosted the wheeled bed through them, I tried to crawl in as well. But one of the men pushed me away. 'No, sorry,' he said.

I stared up at him with disbelief and whined a little in my throat. I'd just got my boy back, and they were taking him away from me?

'Stay, Bailey. It's OK,' the boy said from inside the truck.

I knew all about Stay. It was my least favourite command! I wriggled in frustration and whined some more as Mum climbed into the truck with Ethan. 'It's OK, Bailey,' she said, and looked up at someone in the crowd. 'Laura? Could you watch Bailey?'

'Sure,' a woman said, and a hand closed around my collar. I knew from the smell that it was Chelsea's mum. She was nice enough, but she wasn't my boy. I pulled a little against her grasp, even though I'd been told to stay.

Dad climbed in to be with Mum and the boy, and the doors of the truck closed. It drove away.

I stared in astonishment and gave a single mournful bark. It was my job to keep the boy safe! How could I do that now? Why didn't these people understand?

Chelsea's mum did not let go. 'Hush, Bailey. It'll be OK,' she whispered. 'They'll be OK.' But I could hear tears in her voice, and I was not reassured.

She took me to one side and stood holding me, while the men with hoses kept spraying until the fire died. All that was left was a choking smell of ash and smoke.

'Has to be arson, no question,' said a man with a flat cap on his head, talking to a woman who'd just arrived in a car and who wore a gun on her belt. I'd learned that people who dressed like this were called police. 'Somebody definitely set this fire,' the man went on. 'The bushes, the tree, all of it went up at once. Family is lucky to be alive.'

'Lieutenant, look at this!' another police officer called.

Chelsea's mother edged up to see what they were all looking at. It was Todd's shoe. I turned my head away guiltily.

'Looks like there's blood on it,' the man said, shining a torch on the shoe and the snow around it.

'The boy got pretty cut up going out of his window,' someone else said.

'Yeah, over there. But not here. All I've got here are dog tracks and this shoe.'

I knew that word 'dog'. Was the word 'bad' going to be said soon? I sank to the soggy ground at Chelsea's mum's feet. Maybe they wouldn't notice me if I made myself very small.

The woman with the gun took the torch and aimed it at the shoe. 'Well, what do you know?' she said. 'OK, you two. See where that trail of blood leads. Sergeant?'

'Yes, ma'am?' a man said, coming closer.

'Keep the traffic off the street and ask those people to move back.'

Chelsea's mother bent down, stroking my head. 'Something wrong, Bailey? You OK?' she asked.

I wagged, but not hard. Nobody was scolding me yet, but maybe they would be soon.

Chelsea's mother froze. She lifted her hand off my fur and looked at it.

'Ma'am, do you live here?' the lieutcnant asked her.

'No. I'm a neighbour.'

'Did you see anyone tonight, anyone at all?'

'No, I was asleep.'

'OK. Could I ask you to join the others over there? Or if you're cold, please just give us your contact information and you can go home.'

'Yes, but . . .' Chelsea's mother said.

'Yes?'

'Could somebody look at Bailey? The dog. I think he's bleeding.'

I wagged again, feeling a bit more hopeful. Nobody seemed interested in Todd's shoe at the moment. Maybe I wasn't in trouble?

The policewoman bent down. 'Are you hurt, boy? How did you get hurt?' she asked. She pointed the torch at me and gently ran her hands over the fur on my throat and around my neck. I licked at her chin. I liked her.

She laughed, but then her face got serious. 'I don't think that's his blood. Ma'am, we'll need to hold on to the dog for a while. Is that OK?'

I was taken over to one of the cars, where a man with scissors snipped off some of my fur, putting it in a plastic bag. 'What do you want to bet it's the same blood type that's on the shoe? I'd say our four-legged friend was on patrol tonight and caught somebody setting a fire,' the woman told the man with the scissors. She ran a hand along my back, and I heard approval in her voice. I wiggled with pleasure and felt my ears and my tail begin to get higher. I was still worried about my boy, but at least nobody seemed about to tell me I'd been a bad dog.

'Lieutenant,' another man said, walking up to us. 'We followed that blood trail. It goes straight to a house about four down. He walked right there and went in at a side door.'

'I'd say we have enough for a search warrant,' the woman said, nodding. 'And I bet that somebody in that house four doors down has a couple of teeth marks in a leg.'

For the next several days, I lived at Chelsea's house. Duchess wanted to play all day long, but I wasn't in a playful mood. I missed the boy. Was he lost again? Was he in trouble? How could I help him if I didn't know where he was? I paced the house restlessly.

Mum showed up on the second day. I ran to the door to greet her and sniffed her all over. I could smell Ethan on her clothes, which made me feel better. I also smelt worry, and tiredness, and a strange, sharp scent that stung my nose and made me shake my head a little.

Even so, the smell of my boy cheered me up, so I played Duchess's favourite game of Tug on the Sock for a while as Mum sat and talked with Chelsea's mum.

'What in the world was that boy doing? Why would he set your house on fire? You could have been killed,' Chelsea's mum said, shaking her head.

'I don't know.' Mum shook her head, too. 'Todd and Ethan used to be friends.'

I turned my head at the sound of Ethan's name. Duchess used the moment to snatch the sock out of my mouth.

'They're sure it's Todd?'

'He confessed when the police took him in for questioning.'

'Did he explain why he did it?'

Duchess shoved the sock into my face, daring me to try to take it away.

'He said he didn't know why he did it.' Mum wrapped both hands around her coffee cup, almost as if it was comforting her.

'Well, for heaven's sake. You know, I always did think that boy was strange. Remember when he pushed Chelsea into the bushes for no reason?'

'No, I never heard that. He pushed her?'

With a sudden lunge, I grabbed the free end of the sock. Duchess dug her feet into the carpet and growled. I pulled her around the room, but she didn't let go.

'Bailey's a hero, now. Todd's leg took eight stitches,' Mum said. When I heard my name, I froze. Duchess did, too. The sock went slack between us. What were the people talking about? Dog biscuits, maybe?

'They want his picture for the paper,' Mum went on.

'Good thing I gave Bailey a bath,' Chelsea's mum said.

So that was what they were talking about? A bath? Not again! I'd just *had* a bath! I spat out the sock. Duchess shook it joyously, prancing around the room in victory.

'How is Ethan?' Chelsea's mum asked.

Mum put her coffee cup down. The boy's name and the flash of worry and grief coming off her made me head straight for her. I put my head in her lap and she stroked my ears. She didn't answer the question.

20

About a week later, Mum came to get me, and she took me on a car ride to a new place called the apartment. This was a small house built into a big building. There were dogs everywhere. Most of them were pretty little, but still kind of interesting. In the afternoons, Mum would take me out to see them in a big cement yard. She would sit on a bench and talk to people while I ran around, making friends and marking territory.

I didn't like the apartment very much. It was small, and it didn't smell like home and, worst of all, the boy wasn't there. Felix the cat was, but that didn't help matters.

Both Dad and Mum left often, and they smelt

like Ethan when they returned, but he wasn't living with us any more – not eating at the table, not lying on the couch, not sleeping in one of the beds. Ethan used to be the one to feed me dinner, and now Mum had to do it. Before the fire, that had been the best part of my day, but now I didn't feel as hungry as I used to. Sometimes I even left food in the bowl.

The strange apartment and the missing boy made my heart ache. I wandered from room to room, especially at night. I didn't want to sleep in a bed without Ethan.

One night, while I was wandering, I poked my nose into a closet and found some boxes sitting there. I could smell something familiar inside one of them, so I got my teeth into a corner, dragged it out, and investigated.

The flip! I'd know that smell anywhere. I got it out and carried it with me when I went back to my wandering. I didn't like the taste or the heavy feeling in my mouth, but I did it for Ethan. When he came back, he'd see that I had been waiting for him.

A few days later, I was lying against the couch, sleepy after a night of carrying the flip from room to room. Felix had curled up against me for a nap, and I could feel his purr – such a giant sound for such a tiny thing – humming against my ribs. Ever since we'd come to the apartment, Felix had seemed to think that I'd become his mother. It was embarrassing, but I'd given up shoving him away. You can't really expect a cat to act like he's got brains.

My ears pricked up a bit when I heard Mum's car drive up outside. I jumped to my feet. Felix blinked at me in bewilderment and yawned as I trotted to the window and put my paws on the sill.

My heart thumped and started racing, as if I'd been running around the yard. It wasn't just Mum getting out of the car. The boy! Ethan was with her!

I couldn't help myself. I was barking and spinning, racing to the door so I could get out to Ethan, racing back to the window so I could watch. Felix panicked and dived under the couch.

When keys jangled in the lock, I was right back at the door, quivering. Mum opened the door a crack. Ethan's smell wafted in. I barked eagerly. My boy! Finally!

'Now, Bailey, get back. Down, Bailey, stay down. Sit.'

Well, I couldn't do *that*. I briefly touched my rear end to the floor and then jumped up again, my tail thrashing at the air. Mum put her hand inside the room and snagged my collar, pushing me back as the door swung wide.

'Hey, Bailey. Hey, boy,' Ethan said.

Mum held me away from the boy as he limped in. He was leaning on two long sticks – later I learned that they were called crutches. He stumped awkwardly over to the couch while I danced and twisted and pulled at my collar, whimpering. Why wasn't Mum letting me go? Why was she keeping me back from my boy? Didn't she know how long I'd been waiting?

At last she released my collar, and I threw myself across the room in one bound, landing in the boy's lap, kissing his face.

'Bailey!' Mum said sternly.

'No, it's OK. Bailey, you are such a doodle dog,' the boy said, a smile easing the lines of exhaustion and pain in his face. 'How are you, huh? I missed you, too, Bailey.'

Every time he spoke my name, I wriggled with happiness. The feel of his hands rubbing through my fur was heaven.

The boy was back!

But over the next few days, I began to understand that even though Ethan had come to live with us again, everything still wasn't right. I could tell from the way he stood and walked and the way his voice sounded that he was in pain. It wasn't just his leg that hurt. A mournful sadness drifted off him, and sometimes a gloomy anger flared when all he was doing was sitting still, looking out of the window.

A few days after Ethan came home, there was a knock on the door, and when Mum opened it, the apartment filled up with boys. 'Hi, Bailey! Hey, Bailey!' they called out. I recognized their smells. They were the boys who used to run up and down on the big field with Ethan, throwing the football back and forth between them.

The boys laughed and talked and shouted and stood around half the day. Mum brought food from the kitchen, and I got a lot of bites, which made me happy. Ethan seemed happy, too. But as soon as the boys had gone, the good feelings inside him drained away.

Ethan got up, using his crutches, and limped into the room where our new bed was. He sat on it, looking out of the window. I followed him and jumped up to look, too. I could see the group of boys leaving the apartment building. They jostled and pushed each other, and one pulled a ball out of his pocket. Another one raced down the pavement and caught the ball easily after the first one threw it as hard as he could.

I could feel grief and anger and helplessness thud into Ethan like a rock. I shoved my head under his arm, but he didn't even lift a hand to pet me.

For some reason, it felt as if we were lost again, out in the woods with nobody near. Then I had known what to do. I'd kept the boy warm, made sure he kept moving. I hadn't let him give up.

How could I do that now?

There was only one thing I could think of. I jumped

down from the bed and nosed about in the corners of all the rooms until I found what I was looking for. I hurried back to Ethan and laid the flip in his lap.

He looked down at it and shook his head. I jumped up on the bed beside him and flopped down, a little whine in my throat. This time he lifted his hand to rub behind my ears, but I could tell that he was no happier.

'My whole life's dream is gone, Bailey. Because of Todd,' Ethan told me.

I didn't understand what he was saying, but there was no mistaking the despair in his voice.

'It's not just football,' he told me. I stirred the tip of my tail in a tiny wag. I recognized that word. Were we going to go back to the big field? It didn't seem as if we were. Ethan didn't budge.

'I can't do anything now,' he said. 'Can't play sports. Can't ride a bike. Can't even run. I can walk. Barely.' His hand tightened for a minute in my fur. 'Because of Todd,' he said again. 'I've got nothing left. Because of Todd.'

The days slowly grew warmer, and tiny leaves came out on the trees. Ethan didn't use his crutches any more. Now he walked with the help of a polished stick called a cane. The cane was very special, and I understood without anyone telling me that I wasn't supposed to chew on it, not even a little.

There came a day with a lot of packing and carrying things out to the car, and then we all got to take a ride back to our old home. Everything looked the same but it smelt different, of fresh wood and paint and wallpaper. I carefully investigated every room, my nose busily working, and then burst through the dog door and into the backyard to let out a bark of joy. Duchess answered from down the street. Home!

Ethan left every morning for school, just as he used to do, but I knew that he was no happier. He was tired when he came home, and his leg ached; I could tell by how heavily he leaned on the cane. He'd go into his room and lie down on the bed. Sometimes he didn't even come out for dinner.

Mum and Dad would sit at the table and talk in low voices. 'Ethan' would be in every other sentence.

Not long after we'd come back to the house, Mum woke Ethan up early one morning, and we all piled into the car for another ride. This time, when we got out, we were at the farm!

I raced around to smell all the familiar smells – Flare in the barn, Grandma's cooking in the kitchen, the wonderful woodsy tang of dirt and leaves and mushrooms and squirrel and rabbit and, off in the distance, skunk.

I ran back out of the woods, waving my tail happily, to find the family all gathered on the porch. 'Don't you want to let Hannah know you're here?' Grandma asked.

My ears pricked up. Hannah? The girl?

'She doesn't want to see me like this,' Ethan answered, not looking at anybody.

'Ethan!' Grandma looked shocked, and I saw her and Mum exchange a glance.

'Don't tell her I'm here,' Ethan said. 'I don't want anybody to know.'

'Honey, just think about it,' Mum said in a coaxing voice.

'Mum, I said don't tell her!' Leaning on his cane, Ethan stumped out towards the sleeping porch. 'My leg hurts. I'm going to lie down for a while.'

I lay next to the boy for a while, since I knew that was my job, but it was hard. All the fantastic farm smells were drifting in through the screened windows of the porch. Both my feet and my tail were twitching. Finally, I couldn't stand it any more. I bounced up and over to the door of the porch, looking back at the boy to see if he would come with me.

'Fine, Bailey.' The boy heaved himself up and opened the door for me. 'You go run,' he said. 'At least one of us can.'

I tore happily around the pasture, sampling one of

the brown piles Flare had left there – it still didn't taste like anything much – and then dashing into the woods for an excellent stick, and flopping down by the fence for a good chew. When I'd bitten the stick to pieces, I started to head back to the house, but something stopped me. I remembered the walks Ethan and I used to take, and I ducked under the rails of the fence and took off down the road.

We used to go this way, together, before Ethan started taking his own car rides, before we went to the football field so often, before Todd and the fire. I trotted along, my nose to the wind, and when I reached a mailbox that sat at the end of a winding driveway, I smelt a familiar smell.

I carefully inspected the post that the mailbox was sitting on, in case other dogs had been there before me. A few had. I lifted my leg and let them know that I'd been there, too.

While I was doing that, a figure came out on to the porch. 'Bailey?' a voice called. 'Bailey, is that you?'

It was her! The girl! I dashed up the driveway and arrived for a good ear scratch. 'You're here?' she asked. 'Then is Ethan . . . ?'

She stood still and looked up the road towards the farm. I nudged her hand with my nose to get her scratching again. Then I gave her a lick and started back home. I'd been away from the boy too long.

'Bailey, wait!' Hannah called, and she came running down the driveway behind me.

It's always good to have company for a walk. Hannah stayed by my side until we reached the farm. I was about to run back to the house when I spotted Ethan on the dock of the pond, sitting by himself. His cane lay by his side.

I ran to him and licked the back of his neck. He jumped, startled. 'What took you so long, huh, Bailey?' he asked. 'Where did you go?'

Hannah stepped on to the dock.

Ethan must have heard her footsteps and felt the old wooden planks shift under her weight. He got up, painfully, awkwardly, clutching his cane.

Hannah stopped.

I was kind of surprised that the two of them didn't do any of that hugging they seemed to like so much. They didn't do any talking, either. They just looked at each other.

I sat down to see what would happen next. There was always the possibility of a dog biscuit somewhere.

'Well,' Hannah said. 'Are you going to kiss me or what?'

Ethan dropped his cane.

I thumped my tail on the dock as they hugged and hugged. So they still liked that game after all.

'I can't believe you didn't even tell me you'd got

here,' Hannah said, with her face against Ethan's shoulder. 'Bailey had to come get me!'

Ethan looked down at me. Slowly, he grinned. It had been months since I'd seen a grin like that on his face.

He jumped into the water.

Hannah shrieked with surprise. I raced to the end of the dock and looked down. The water was sloshing. Bubbles were rising. At last – at last! – I knew just what to do.

I leaped into the water after my boy.

In no time at all, I had the collar of his shirt in my mouth. I tugged him up to the surface, and we broke into the air. Hannah was sitting down on the dock, laughing.

'I can swim!' Ethan shouted, laughing, too, shaking the water out of his hair. 'I can still swim!'

I was so happy I paddled hard for the little sandy beach by the dock, climbed out, and chased the ducks around the pond.

That night, Ethan and I went to bed out on the porch, the way we always did at the farm. I lay with my head on my boy's chest, and his hand, heavy and sleepy, came up to stroke my head.

'Good dog, Bailey,' he murmured.

For the first time in a long, long time, I could tell my boy was happy.

A DOG'S PURPOSE

Ellie's Story

W. Bruce Cameron

Ellie is a very special dog with a very important
purpose. From puppyhood Ellie has been trained as a
search-and-rescue dog. She can track down a lost child
in a forest or an injured victim under a fallen building.
She finds people. She saves them. It's what she was
meant to do. But Ellie's handlers, Jakob and Maya, need
her too. People can be lost in many ways, and Ellie
needs to find a way to save the people she loves best.